MW01119549

DISCARD

SPIRIT OF A BEAR

Also by the Author

Colorado Ransom

SPIRIT OF A BEAR

Susan Harmon

Walker and Company
New York

First published in the United States of America in 1994 by Walker
Publishing Company, Inc.

Published simultaneously in Canada by Thomas Allen & Son Canada,
Limited, Markham, Ontario

Library of Congress Cataloging-in-Publication Data
Harmon, Susan.
Spirit of a bear / Susan Harmon.
p.   cm.
ISBN 0-8027-4140-1
1. Frontier and pioneer life—Colorado—Fiction.   2. Women
pioneers—Colorado—Fiction.   3. Ute Indians—Fiction.   I. Title.
PS3558.A62457S65   1994   94-3016
CIP

Printed in the United States of America

2   4   6   8   10   9   7   5   3   1

This book is dedicated to those courageous women who helped settle the American West.

SPIRIT OF A BEAR

CHAPTER 1

ONLY A FEW men still lingered at the Wet Whistle, a favorite watering hole of the miners who frequented the place. At the bar were three miners. One was cleaning his nails with a short-bladed knife. One tugged constantly at his left earlobe as he watched a card game in progress over in the corner by the stove. The third was busy trying to keep his pipe going.

"Bad batch of tobacco, Trap?" Ben Barnes asked, momentarily shaking his bad mood. The saloon keeper hardly listened for the answer. His mulligrubs over the loss of the long, warm summer evenings that brought men to his saloon with regularity and kept them drinking for hours after their day in the mines were affecting his concentration. Of course, his establishment was frequently damaged as a result of a fight or even a brawl. Now, he almost wished one of the gents at the poker table in the corner would catch another slipping a card up his sleeve just so the place would liven up a bit.

Eventually, the nail cleaner and the earlobe tugger got up and ambled out. Trap McRae had finally got his pipe going, making the room smell worse than a bear's den in early spring.

With a sigh, Ben quit polishing glasses, tossed his rag under the counter, poured himself a shot of his best whiskey, and strode down the bar to where Trap sat nursing his pipe.

The two remained silent for a few minutes—the short, rotund man with a bald, shiny pate surrounded by a sparse, almost white fringe and the somewhat younger

1

man of perhaps forty, with dark, slightly graying, shoulder-length hair, his big, coarse hands clutching at his pipe.

"I sure dread these long winter nights," Ben said to break the silence.

"Yep, me too," Trap replied. "I expect they'll start makin' my feet itch."

"Yeah, I hadn't thought of that," Ben said.

Thornton McRae used to make his living as a trapper, one of the last to do so. Trap would leave towns far behind in the late fall to seek the rich winter pelt of the beaver along the mountain streams. Each year beaver grew more scarce, but he had managed to make a living in the trade and had supplemented his income with a little prospecting until an unfriendly bout with a few Indians the previous year. He had been caught in one of his own traps after it had been moved by some Arapaho who had an evil intent against him. Nursing a severe leg wound, he had barely made it back to Elk Fork in time to stop a gangrenous infection that threatened him with the loss of his leg. As he recovered slowly, he decided to try his fortune in the mining business, at least until his wounds healed. He still got around with a heavy limp. And his spirits were still healing.

Fall was a rough time for Trap. When he thought about the snow swirling through the big trees in the back country, he could almost feel the soft thickness of a beaver pelt in his fingers. But the realities of a regular paycheck from S & S Mining Company and his seriously disabling limp overrode his desire to return to his former occupation for the time being.

"Ben, you need to get something in here to liven this place up a little," he said as he drained his second whiskey. He dreaded going back to his cabin, five miles outside of town. Four walls still gave him a feeling of claustrophobia.

"Yeah, Trap, I reckon I do." Ben leaned his forearms on the counter and swirled his glass between both hands.

"Maybe I could find me a lively piano player. That might do the trick."

"Girls."

"What's that you say?"

"Girls. You need some girls in here."

Ben straightened up quickly. "Girls? You mean sportin' women?"

"Naw, I meant Sunday School teachers! Of course, sportin' women is the kind of girls I meant. That'd keep these miners out of their cold beds a mite later at night." Just the thought of a woman made him ache for the Indian woman he had left in the mountains with her people.

Ben narrowed his eyes, thinking about the prospect. "It would pick up business; it would surely do that. But where would we get any women? There's not more'n a dozen white women in these hills around here, and they've all got husbands, all except Widow Simpson."

"There must be plenty of men around that knows a workin' girl somewhere down their backtrail that they could talk into comin' up here. Let's ask the boys in the corner what they think of the idea. Looks like their game is breakin' up anyway."

The four cardplayers gathered around at Trap's bidding. With a free nightcap from Ben, they all expressed support for the idea, slapping each other on the back with delight.

Soon a cheerful banter had erupted spontaneously from the group who had sat silently in the corner for three hours or more.

"We're forgettin' something," Ben said. "We've got respectable women living hereabouts. They'd never stand for such a thing. I'd better just stick to the idea of gettin' a piano player."

"A piano player!" one of the men said. "Who wants a piano player when there's no girls to dance with?"

The men noisily hooted in agreement.

Trap spoke up quietly, but convincingly, "What are the women gonna do, Ben? They'll raise hell with their men, but their husbands don't hardly give you no business anyway, and you don't have a woman you have to go home and answer to. The women will fuss and gripe and pray over it for a few weeks, but then they'll get onto somethin' else and forget about your girls. Besides, you're the mayor here. You got to handle business as best you see fit for the town."

That just about convinced Ben. "Well, maybe it could work out. Give me some time to think on it." As the men filed out, Ben envisioned his place filled with miners, gambling and drinking the frigid nights away and dancing with pretty, buxom women.

Word about Ben's plans spread quickly through the mines the next day. That evening, right after quitting time, the miners besieged the Wet Whistle like a cloud of locusts upon a Kansas wheat field. No man wanted to lose the opportunity to encourage Ben. It was one of Ben's most profitable nights in the history of the saloon.

Soon the pockets in Ben's big apron were stuffed with little shreds of paper on which the men had printed the names of their favorite dance-hall girls and the names of the towns where they had last been working. Ben's spirits were soaring, and, as a wise businessman, he knew he should try to harness some of their enthusiasm for his new project. He grabbed a poker from underneath the stove and beat it loudly against the big iron monstrosity to draw everyone's attention.

"Gents, we gotta get this thing organized. I'm gonna need some help with this project so's we can get a few of these women here before snow comes and closes all the trails."

The men's voices rose in agreement.

Through the clamoring crowd, walked a man who towered over most of those present. His broad shoulders stood out in a room full of muscular miners. He had a rugged face framed by a shock of dark red, bristly hair. A star was pinned to his chest.

The crowd quietened some as he moved among them to his brother, Ben, standing by the stove. "What you organizing, Ben? I'm outta town for a couple of days and come back to the biggest party this town's ever seen except for maybe the Fourth of July. Guess I missed some excitement. What's happenin'?"

Ben tried to explain, but his voice was drowned out by the excited voices of the other men.

From the words and phrases he could pick out from the rowdy crowd, Sheriff Red Barnes figured out the general idea of his brother's plans. He held up his hand for silence with a good-natured grin on his face.

"I think I get it. My brother here has recruited you to help him get some women in this establishment. Well, you men go on with your party, but I need to talk to Ben for a while."

Nothing on the sheriff's face told the men in the crowd what Ben could pick up in a sharp glance from his brother. He knew Red was mad. Ben led the way quickly to his living quarters in the back of the saloon before anyone could detect the animosity.

As soon as the door was shut, Red's smile faded. "Dammit, Ben, what has got hold of you? Where did you get the idea to bring women in here?"

Ben walked over to a corner of the room and sat down in a chair before a glowing stove that was a smaller replica of the big wood burner in the saloon.

"Well, Red, the idea just sort of come up last night when a few of us was talkin' about some way to liven up the place during winter. Business is fallin' off. And when the nights get colder it'll no doubt get worse, just like last winter. I don't know how I can get through another year like that."

He paused and took a deep breath. "What's the harm of it? We've got lots of lonely men around here."

"We've also got a fairly peaceful little town here! The men don't have much to get riled up over except a card game gone sour now 'n then. You want to bring in a bunch of women for them to fight over?" His voice was loud, but he made sure it could not be heard over the noise from the saloon. "Listen to them out there. That's a crazy bunch you've got. And, Ben, that's just with the *thought* of women. Do you know how much worse it can get?" He paused for a moment to let his words sink in.

Ben frowned, but did not reply.

"Ben, I've sheriffed in towns where there's saloon women, and I tell you, I ain't goin' to do it again."

"But, Red, it seems to me that it might have a beneficial effect on the men here. There's mighty few women around—"

"That's the point," Red interrupted. "What women we've got here are respectable, and for you to try to flaunt a bunch of saloon girls in their faces is downright outrageous!"

Red stomped out, leaving Ben to ponder.

Ben found out the following night just how outrageous the women thought the idea was.

Close to the miners' quitting time, he had his glasses lined up on the bar and the whiskey bottles ready to pour. A keg of beer was open and another ready to haul out when needed. He was just giving the bar its last swipe and watching the clock in anticipation of the rush when he noticed three women crossing the street, which was still muddied from the early snow of two nights ago.

The women were not picking up their skirts and daintily sidestepping the oozy spots as ladies usually did. Hooked together arm-in-arm, they walked staunchly toward the Wet Whistle.

Ben was alarmed momentarily by the prospect of respectable women trying to walk into his establishment.

His worries in that regard were needless. The women made no effort to enter. When they reached the doors, they stopped, turned around, and still arm-in-arm, faced the street.

Ben watched as they were joined by other women, arriving separately or by twos or threes. Without so much as a hello to each other, they all interlocked their arms and stood facing the street. Soon there were a dozen women lined up outside with their overcoats on and their heads warmly wrapped in scarves. Even the Widow Simpson had shown up.

Ben positioned himself slightly out of sight, where he could keep an eye on the women and one on the street. Whenever a man came in sight of the saloon and saw the formidable lineup outside, he would turn tail as fast as a hound dog facing an angry skunk.

Ben spent a sad night alone watching the women standing there as the sun went down, the moon came up, and the stars began to show themselves. Ben finally put the bottles back on their shelves, closed up the keg of beer—hoping it was not yet too flat to serve on some other occasion—and turned off his lights. By then the women had gone home, but he did peep out one last time to satisfy himself before going to bed.

Ben rose early the next morning, eager to go outside and inspect his establishment for damage. He knew women could seem soft as a spring cloud one moment, then suddenly burst forth like a raging thunderhead the next; the women he had seen in front of the Wet Whistle had seemed anything but soft. The morning perusal of the premises showed nothing out of the ordinary. Inside, he stared with regret at the keg of beer, kicked it in passing, and felt angered that he had probably wasted the $12.35 it had cost him just because of a bunch of indignant women.

No customers entered the bar that day. But there was an appreciable rise in bottled sales to men who came calling at his backdoor. With every bottle that he sold, however, Ben calculated how much more he could have received if the bottle had been sold drink by drink.

Fortunately, at nightfall only a half-dozen women appeared, as silent as before, but still apparently as staunch.

Through the next few days, Ben hardly left his establishment and saw few people from the community except for the occasional patron arriving at his backdoor and stealing away quietly as soon as his purchase was made. Even his brother stayed clear. There had been no more snow, but Ben found himself praying for a two- or three-footer because he figured the women would not venture out in drifts that would plunge them up to their thighs. Finally, on the fifth day of the standoff, Ben got his storm, but it brought no comfort to him when he saw the women stalking through the snow, wearing their men's old trousers underneath their skirts. He immediately turned off the lights, retreated to his bedroom, and lay in bed, tapping his fingers on his chest until he finally fell asleep.

The next morning, he knew he had to confront the situation. The few men he had questioned as they slipped rather furtively through the backdoor to purchase a bottle or two could give him no information. They were single men. He knew he had to hear from a family man. Before the sun was high in the sky, he threw on his overcoat and began trudging through the snow, which was almost up to his knees.

The sheriff's office stood facing the main street of Elk Fork, which was just about the only street the town had. Smoke poured out of the stovepipe above the little gray building, making Ben hopeful that his brother would have hot coffee to offer him.

He shoved the door open and found his brother studiously going through a pile of paperwork on the desk, a steaming cup of coffee in front of him. The tiny office, with a couple of cells beyond, was warm and inviting to Ben after his chilly walk. He tried to show his stormy mood by not speaking up right away. He just stood there, beating his boots against the door frame to rid them and his pants legs of the powdery snow that clung to them.

Red did little more than glance up from his stack of papers and say briefly, "Mornin', Ben, come in and pour yourself a cup of coffee."

Ben entered, slamming the door behind him, and leaving little white piles of moisture on the floor as he advanced toward the stove.

"Mornin', Red. Why haven't you been over to see me the last few days?"

"Been afraid of those guards of yours, I guess," Red said, still poring over the papers on his desk.

"Dammit, Red, what's botherin' these women anyhow?"

Red finally looked up, pushing his paperwork aside. "I guess you riled 'em with that talk of yours about bringing in saloon women."

"But who told 'em? I didn't think they would find out till after the women were here."

"You know damned well that with as many men as you had in your saloon the other night, lathered up over the prospects of women, a person would have to be blind and deaf not to find out that bit of news!"

"You're my brother. Why don't you get over there and help me defend my business?"

"Defend it against what?"

"Dammit, you're the sheriff here. You knew those women have been lining up in front of my place every night! Why haven't you done something about it?" Ben felt he was boiling almost as much as the steamy coffeepot sitting on the stove.

"Ben, those women were just standing there! They didn't make any threats to anybody that I heard of. Did they threaten to kill you or one of your customers? Did they come at anybody with a shootin' iron or brass knuckles? Did they try to burn you out?" Red was getting a little steamed up, too. Besides, he had been glad to see the women unite to dissuade his brother from carrying out what he thought was a piss-poor idea.

"Red, those females have been interferin' with private enterprise. It's my right to make a livin' in this town; after all, I'm the mayor here! What the hell are we gonna do?"

"We, Mr. Mayor, Your Honor, are going to do nothing. What you do with your business is up to you!" Red turned and opened up the belly of the stove to shove another couple of logs into it.

Ben stared out the window, fuming. He wanted to storm out and leave his brother, but he thought better of it. He figured he needed Red's support, so he choked back his pride.

"Red, do you have any suggestions for me? My business has just gone to hell!" His voice rose in desperation.

"Well, Ben, I will admit that I've been thinking about your problem. I could get the word out that you didn't mean it about gettin' women in there, that it has been a big misunderstanding. I could do that if you make me a promise that it's forgot about."

Ben was a sorry loser. He turned toward his brother, "I'm the mayor of this town, and if I want a few women in my establishment, you can't stop me."

Red looked at him hard. "No, I can't stop you if you are determined to do that. But I'm not the one who's costing you business by driving off your customers every night."

Ben thought about that comment for a while, warming his hands around his coffee cup and staring at the floor. Then he got on to what he had really come to ask about. "What does Betsy think?"

Betsy was Red's wife, a pretty, sharp-spoken woman some fifteen years younger than Red. Betsy kept in close touch with the few women around Elk Fork, attending all the sewing bees and quilting parties with her and Red's two toddlers in tow.

"Betsy's madder than a wet hen. Don't expect to be invited to Sunday dinner for a while."

"Has she told you what the women are sayin'?"

"She don't have to tell me, or tell you either. You know what they're sayin'! I expect they'll stand out in front of the Wet Whistle all winter if that's what it takes to make you give up your danged plans. Why, I've nearly had to chain her to the cookstove to keep her from joinin' them herself!"

"I never thought they would be so stubborn."

"Don't know why you didn't. These are plucky women we've got out here. If they wasn't, they wouldn't be out here in the middle of the wilderness."

Ben began to feel that the situation was becoming hopeless. Already his pocketbook was beginning to feel flatter than a stepped-on cow pie.

Red could read the expression on his brother's face, so he repeated his offer. "I could get the word out about a misunderstanding—if you promise to forget the idea."

"You think that would do the trick and get them women off my back?"

Red sighed and said, "It's worth a try."

The female patrol in front of the Wet Whistle promptly ended, and Ben's business began to pick up. Still, things did not seem quite right to Ben.

He saw his brother now and then, but talk was limited to the weather and other minor topics. He started to get the feeling that Red was still upset with him, but decided to just act indifferent for a few days and see if his brother came around to being his old self.

It was an unusually warm and sunny day when Red suddenly started to act as if his feelings toward Ben had thawed out, too. Ben was outside sweeping slush off the boardwalk and occasionally taking a swipe at a melting icicle still hanging from the roof. Red walked up and absently stomped his boots a couple of times right where Ben had just swept.

"Howdy, Ben. Let's go in and have a little snort."

Ben set his broom to one side and followed Red indoors. He pulled a bottle of fair-to-middlin' whiskey off the shelf, poured them each a shot, and set a cup of bitter-smelling coffee beside each glass.

Red was not quick to speak. He took off his hat and laid it on the counter, and Ben could see the little furrow that ran parallel across Red's forehead when there was something on his mind. When Red got really upset about something, the furrow developed to slanty lines on either end that ran nearly to his hairline. Ben was relieved to see that those lines were not visible today. Red ran his fingers through his scruffy mane where his hat had plastered it close to his scalp.

"Betsy asked me to come by and see if you'd take Sunday dinner with us day after tomorrow."

"She wantin' to make peace, is she?"

Red looked up from studying the grounds swirling on the top of his coffee. "She ain't the one to be needin' to make peace, Ben. She ain't done no wrong. You comin' to dinner or not?"

"Now, Red, don't get testy. I just don't think her or any other of these women around here got a right to interfere in a man's business is all." Ben stopped short when he saw a shadow of a line flash upward on Red's forehead. He tried quickly to cover his error. "But after all, I guess it's for the good of the community. I just got to keep remindin' myself of that. Yeah, tell Betsy I'll be there and that I appreciate her invitation. I'll be there about noon."

Red seemed to relax a little then, and the two of them went on to talk of other things. Ben wondered if he could still sense a tension in the way Red held his shoulders, but looking forward to Betsy's cooking, he shrugged off the thought.

CHAPTER 2

BEN DID WITHOUT breakfast on Sunday morning, just drinking a little coffee as he swept the cigarette butts out of the saloon and cleaned up a few fragments of glass that had ended up on the floor during a fracas between several miners. It almost seemed like spring, a sunny morning that could have been hand-delivered by God and a healthy brawl the night before. Ben thought with pride that his was probably the only saloon within a good hundred miles that had an honest-to-God wooden floor instead of dirt or sawdust, although it did pain him when he saw the splatters of tobacco juice. He hauled out a bucket of soapy water and a stiff brush and tackled the malodorous stains. Thoughts of perhaps a pecan pie or jelly doughnuts at Betsy's made the chore more pleasant.

Close to noon, Ben dressed in a clean white shirt, dark gray pants, and a lighter gray vest to call on his brother's family. The day was warm, so he didn't bother with his topcoat, which was slightly spattered with mud around the hem.

Betsy greeted him warmly, almost as if nothing had happened. The children, Bobby and Sam, climbed on and off his lap, tugged at his pants legs, and untied his boots while Betsy placed the meal on the table. The house smelled warmly of yeast, and Ben could hardly wait for dessert.

The meal was finished and Ben was almost salivating in expectation of the sweets when he began to be suspicious as Betsy announced, "I'm expecting company. Why don't we wait for them to join us for dessert. I'll just put on another pot of coffee."

Ben looked at Red, but saw merely a slight furrowing of the brow as he would expect Red to exhibit at the thought of any of Betsy's church people coming to visit. Ben made do with another cup of coffee and tried to get his mind off the expected visitors by playing horsey with Bobby and Sam. As he juggled them alternately upon his knees, he weighed the prospect of foregoing dessert. He would miss the doughnuts and the chocolate pies that were sitting on the table if he made up an excuse to go back to the Wet Whistle. Or he could steel himself to tolerate Betsy's church friends and enjoy the sweets.

He decided upon the latter. Then the minister of the little church led a procession of four women to Betsy's front door.

During the week, Brother Herman Glover was the driving force behind a pick and shovel over at the S&S Mining Company, close to Wet Wash Pass. But come Sundays and holidays, Brother Glover changed into a black suit with shiny spots at the knee and elbow, slicked down his hair with some kind of loud-smelling oil, and let go with his spiritual orations with the same strength and fervor that he vented on the pick and shovel through the week. It seemed his energy was unlimited, although spread in widely divergent directions.

When Betsy opened the door, Brother Glover gave a formal bow, sweeping a worn felt hat forward as he allowed the four women who accompanied him to enter. After the ladies removed their coats, introductions were made as a mere formality. Ben had never taken an interest in the women of Elk Fork because they were all married and none had ever passed a dime over his counter. Their names passed over him as he nodded his head toward each of them and smiled absently. The only one he knew was Widow Simpson.

In greeting, Mrs. Simpson reached toward Ben with her gloved hand and a coy smile on her wrinkled face. Ben grasped her hand reluctantly and mumbled a few words that he hoped were appropriate. As soon as possible, Ben scuttled back to his chair in front of the fireplace and gathered the two boys into his lap. To his chagrin, the women and Brother Glover also settled themselves in front of the fire, crowding on either side of him. Ben had hoped the women would take off to the kitchen to be with Betsy. Instead, they began to chatter about church things, of which Ben knew little.

Within ten minutes, Ben started to feel the sweat trickle down his chest and spine; even his boots grew moist and swishy inside. The company of Widow Simpson had always had this effect upon him, and now it was multiplied fourfold by the presence of her companions. Even Bobby and Sam seemed intimidated. They settled quietly onto their uncle's lap and leaned against his chest, their eyes darting from one to another of their visitors.

One of the ladies turned to Ben with a direct look. He froze as he realized she was about to speak directly to him.

"Mr. Barnes, since you are mayor of this town, duly elected by our menfolk, don't you think it would become your position to attend church on Sunday as do many of those men who elected you?"

Ben sat up straight, cuddling the boys close to his chest as though for his own protection. "Ma'am, as you must have already seen, I have not been bestowed with a good sense of the social graces." It was a sentence Ben had practiced in his mind many times because he knew sooner or later it would be needed. He hoped she would smile at him and not pursue the matter, so he smiled politely at her.

She was not so easily repressed. "You do worship the Lord, Mayor Barnes?"

"I do, ma'am. In the privacy of my home, I read the Bible and pray regularly." In the back of his mind, he began a prayer right now that the Lord would deliver him from the sharp questioning of this intense woman.

"Well, it seems to me if you spend all those nights in the accompaniment of the patrons of your establishment, you might spare two hours a week in the company of respectable folk." She lifted her hand haughtily and, with her little finger, smoothed her right eyebrow while gazing out the window as if to distance herself from Ben Barnes and his ideas of holiness.

Ben sat up a little straighter, preparing himself to defend the subtle charge that the patrons of the Wet Whistle were not respectable.

Brother Glover cut in, "Ben, maybe Mrs. Taylor's comments bring us to the real purpose of this little get-together today."

"Purpose?" Ben croaked. "I thought this was a social call."

"Well, it is, Ben, but it has another purpose, too." Brother Glover leaned forward, his elbows on his knees. "Ben, we took great offense to your recent idea regarding womenfolk in your place of business," he began delicately.

Ben considered bolting for the door, but he noticed that his brother had placed himself there, leaning against the wooden frame and picking his teeth with a match stem.

"Brother Glover, say no more." Ben knew it would do no good to use the excuse of the misunderstanding that he and Red had come up with. "You and the ladies, of course, were offended and righteously so," Ben said, trying to compose himself and speak in his best mayoral tone. "I don't know what came over me to have had such a disgusting idea. Now, why don't we just forget about this nonsense. Believe me, I have learned my lesson." Ben hoped he sounded contrite enough to assuage the feelings of the ladies and the preacher.

"Now, Ben, simmer down. We are not here to rake you over the coals about your mistake."

"You're not?"

"No, we're not. We know you showed poor judgment,

but you may have brought our attention to a problem that is eating like rot in our little community, keeping our men from knowing the full glory of life." His voice was beginning to take on the pulpit singsong that replaced his everyday speech of a simple miner.

Ben was puzzled. "Glory of life?"

"Yes, Brother Ben, the glory that a man can only feel when he has a woman by his side, and the glory that a woman can only feel when she has a mate by her side. These simple miners are seeking solace in your establishment, in the bottle and at the card tables, to make up for the emptiness in their lives that only a wife and family can fill. We are beholden to you, Brother Ben, for calling our attention to the wasteland that these poor men face each day when their labor is done."

"Wasteland?" Ben felt he was beginning to sound like a parrot he had once seen in a carnival sideshow.

"Yes, a wasteland of loneliness, sin, and drunkenness. And only two things can bring the men of our community to salvation. One answer, of course, is clear—the Lord." Brother Glover arose and walked around behind his chair, leaning over the back of it as if it were a pulpit. "But it is not easy to bring these men of ours to the Lord without the help of the gentler sex, without the help of women. These men need women to point them toward the path of righteousness!"

Ben could not help but interrupt. "What are you talkin' about?" He turned toward Red, who was still standing beside the door. "What's he talkin' about, Red?" Ben pulled a handkerchief from his pocket and wiped his moist forehead.

Red merely shrugged and said, "Just listen to the man, Ben."

Brother Glover stood leaning across the chair, eyes snapping from face to face as if he were before a congregation. "Brother Ben, don't you see? These men here need womenfolk in their lives. Not the kind you were going to use to finish wrecking their souls, but the kind of women like our sisters here." He nodded individually to the women present. "The men need wives, Ben, and you are going to be the instrument of the Lord to see that they get them!"

Ben looked toward Red again, but got no notice.

Before Ben could speak, Brother Glover continued, "We are going to bring salvation to these men here in Elk Fork, you and me and these ladies here. We're going to advertise for wives for these needful miners of ours!"

As though in a daze, Ben trudged through the crusty snow back to the Wet Whistle late that afternoon, trying to make sense of a world that suddenly seemed to have gone topsy-turvy. He tried to bridge the huge gap between the prospect of bringing in two or three sporting women to this befuddling notion of arranging for brides. It seemed to him that these few church women and that silver-tongued preacher had the men's lives all planned out for them. The miners had not even been consulted. Who knew if even one of them wanted a wife? If they did, Ben reasoned, the mountains were full of Indian women to be had for the price of a couple of good horses. He recalled that Brother Glover had said something about a special sermon in church next Sunday, to be followed by a potluck dinner supplied by the women of the church and what the preacher had called an organizational meeting.

"Huh! He'd be preachin' to an empty house if it wasn't for the Sunday dinner the women will be fixin'," Ben muttered to himself angrily as he entered the Wet Whistle and struck a match to the lantern hanging beside the door. His big orange cat, DC, a name shortened from his frequent references to the damned cat, was sitting at his usual place on the end of the bar. DC stood up and began to stretch when Ben walked in. Ben ignored him, although he knew he had forgotten to put out any food for him earlier in the day. Ben grabbed the poker and a couple of logs and began stoking the fire in the potbellied stove.

It wasn't long before Trap walked in. "Where you been all day? I got a little thirsty waitin' for you to open up." Trap leaned against the bar and smoothed his mustache while he waited for Ben to pour his drink.

"Oh, just been over at my brother's place."

"His wife on speakin' terms with you now?" Trap tried not to grin. Everybody in Elk Fork knew about the cold shoulder Betsy had been showing toward her brother-in-law.

"Yup," Ben replied shortly, kicking at the cat that was twining itself through Ben's legs in an attempt to remind him of supper.

"You seem a little out of sorts. Things not go well with Betsy?"

"I don't know, Trap. I just don't know." He poured himself a big slug from the bottle that he had placed on the counter in front of Trap.

Soon the drink had him talking. He related the afternoon's events to Trap, feeling somewhat better now that he could talk about it and try to get it into some kind of perspective.

"What have I started, Trap?" he questioned as he ended the story.

"You want my opinion? It might not be such a bad idea. Now, I hate to side with the church ladies, and I ain't too fond of Herman Glover either, but there just might be something to this. I left a Indian woman up in the mountains with her people. We had us a little boy. I miss that woman and the boy. I didn't spend a lot of time with 'em, but I always knowed they was there. Lots of these men hereabouts might be better off if they had a woman to come home to."

"But think what it would do to my business if all the men

got married. Maybe they'd be better off, Trap, but what about my business?"

"Branch out, Ben. You'd prob'ly do better if you built a general store alongside this saloon. Town needs one."

Ben looked at Trap for a minute or two, thinking about what he had just said. "You may have somethin' there, Trap. This town's growin'. Maybe it is time for a store here, and some weddin's will mean a few kids, whole new families, in no time." Ben rubbed his nose absently, lost in thought about the idea of expanding his business.

On the Saturday night before the big Sunday dinner, there was a good-sized crowd in the Wet Whistle. The men were drinking up, looking forward to the big feed on Sunday. Ben was too busy at the bar to catch more than a few words of conversation here and there, but he could sense that a few of the men were taking some ribbing because they were seriously considering Brother Glover's idea, which Ben still considered preposterous. He was disappointed when the men began sauntering out early, obviously not wanting to be too hung over to get to the Sunday gathering.

As he frequently did, Trap stayed after the others left. Ben usually figured he was lonesome and wanted to talk, although sometimes he just wanted to sit in silence for a while, nursing a whiskey.

Ben sauntered down the bar to feel out if Trap wanted to talk.

"Goin' to the services tomorrow, Ben?"

"Well, I figured that as mayor, maybe I ought to be there. Besides, Betsy won't be home to cook dinner. I might as well eat at the church. How about you?" Ben guffawed at the ridiculous nature of his own question.

Trap hesitated before answering, "Well, I just might."

Ben looked at Trap with a smile, figuring he was teasing.

"Well, if you're gonna be there, I ain't goin'. Ain't gonna take a chance on lightning strikin' the church."

Trap shrugged. "Do as you please. I figger I got a right to go."

Ben could see that his joke had fallen flat, and he didn't want to hurt the feelings of one of his best customers. "Sure, Trap, I was just kiddin'. It's just that you ain't any more of a churchgoin' man than I am, but it is goin' to be a good feed. Don't blame ya for wantin' to go." To make amends, Ben poured him another whiskey. "On the house," he said in a rare gesture of generosity.

"It ain't just the food, Ben," Trap responded with a nod of appreciation as he sipped at the fresh drink. "I been doin' some thinkin'. I ain't gettin' any younger, and this stove-up leg don't seem to be improvin' much. Ever' time we have a cold spell, my ankle goes plum' stiff on me. It seems like I might as well forget about goin' back to the mountain life. I might just as well figger on settlin' down. If I gotta do that, a woman might be a comfort, where I could come home to a warm house and a good supper."

Ben had never seen Trap so morose; he put it down to too much whiskey and decided to humor him. "You thinkin' about takin' a wife, then?" Ben stifled a smile.

"Thinkin' on it. These gents who've been talkin' about it can make it sound purty good."

"Aw, shucks, Trap. They're just tryin' to urge each other on, kind of a dare."

"I ain't so sure, Ben." Trap slugged down the last of his drink and headed for the door. "Don't be surprised if you see me at the churchhouse tomorrow." He stopped at the door and turned back briefly. "Mountain life was good while it lasted and I had a good woman, but it can't last forever."

Ben shook his head, figuring Trap would probably not even remember their conversation the next day.

As Ben sat by himself that night he had to admit that he

had seriously misjudged the men's amorous desires. Although the excitement did not match the passion the men had shown when the prospect of saloon women had been introduced, Ben had seen the enthusiasm building as the men gathered around the hand-printed notices that Brother Glover had nailed all over the little town to announce the special services on Sunday. Large printing noted that the sermon would be "Hearth and Home: God's Special Gift." A partial menu of the special dishes to be prepared by the ladies of the church followed.

By morning, Ben's curiosity got the better of him, and he dressed in his best to represent the office of the mayor of Elk Fork.

The little church, which Herman Glover had built practically alone, was filled to capacity. A few men even crowded about in the chilly air of the tiny front porch to listen through the open door as Brother Glover made an impassioned plea for the men to open their hearts to receive the blessings of marriage. Of course, Brother Glover, being single himself, set the example, declaring to the congregation in a dramatic fashion that he had a strong desire to obtain the hand of a lady in marriage. He urged the men who also were so inclined to meet with him after the services.

In truth, Herman Glover was a lonely man and had for some time considered leaving the mountains to seek a more social life in the eastern states, but a thought had struck him. Rather than leave the mountains he so loved and leave a fairly prosperous job in a town where he was well respected, why not bring a woman here? This idea was spawned by the rumors of Ben Barnes's plan to import saloon women for the purpose of furthering his business. Instead, Glover would import respectable women for the purpose of marriage—to him and to anyone else who liked the idea.

Herman Glover was a sincere man, but one who was

strongly tempted by worldly ways. Many a night he lay awake, alone in his bed, and thought of his friends engaged in the sinful conduct of cardplaying and im-imbibing of spirits down at the Wet Whistle, and he prayed for forgiveness because he was sorely tempted to join them.

Ben had doubted Brother Glover's sincerity, but became profoundly aware of the man's earnestness somewhere about halfway through the hour-long sermon. Brother Glover's face took on a look that was beseeching, yet at the same time exuding a powerful force which seemed to pervade the room. As those in the congregation, both men and women, burst forth now and then with a shout of "Hallelujah!" or "Praise the Lord!" Ben felt an uncanny urge to do the same. As he felt his will seeming to melt into and become a part of the minister's compelling force, he began to wish he had not attended the service.

At the end of the sermon, Ben arose at the preacher's bidding when Brother Glover announced, "And, brothers and sisters, I want to honor our mayor, Ben Barnes, for his leadership in this community." Ben felt himself turning red, but managed a little dip of a bow toward the congregation.

As soon as the service was over, several of the single men rushed up to shake Brother Glover's hand. Ben felt his mouth almost drop open when he saw Thornton McRae among them. He had not even seen Trap arrive. "Must've been standing on the porch all this time," Ben muttered to himself, in disbelief as he moseyed over toward the tables set up outside in spite of the chill in the air. He was in such a state of surprise at seeing Trap actually show up that he had almost lost his appetite.

At this point, Herman Glover was not entirely sure how he would accomplish the feat of actually finding marriageable women and enticing them to come to Elk Fork to join in holy matrimony with the six men who had come forth to commit themselves to such a union. But he was sure the Lord would provide a way.

Also, he had a brother who was an attorney in Boston; perhaps Morgan could help him arrive at a solution.

CHAPTER 3

MORGAN GLOVER RECEIVED his brother's letter a few weeks after Herman's victorious sermon in Elk Fork. Morgan had always admired his brother's religious virtue, but he had never shared Herman's zeal for the spiritual. Morgan's Boston law practice was flourishing, and he felt this degree of success would give him an opportunity to add some dignity to his brother's quest for marriageable women. He could certainly identify with the desire for women more readily than he could with his brother's strict religious life. In fact, he hoped this was a sign that his brother might be on the road to becoming a little more closely in tune with the ordinary man.

Morgan immediately called in an employee and set the young man to work inquiring as to means and costs of passage and drafting newspaper advertisements. Morgan leaned back, put his expensive boots on his desk, and reflected that perhaps an additional direction for his business might have been revealed to him. Then he set about designing new stationery that would read *Morgan Glover & Associates, Confidential Marriage Brokers.*

About this same time, Ben Barnes began plans for an extension onto the building that housed the saloon. After Trap's hint to him regarding a general store, he reasoned that if women were coming into town, they would be appalled by the furnishings in the homes supplied by their men. Since it would be well into spring before the addition to his establishment could be completed, he roped off the northeast corner of the saloon and began to fill it slowly

26

with bolts of cloth, boxes of lamps and cookware, fluffy feather pillows, and handmade quilts. It was difficult to obtain these items in winter, when trips down to the settlements were kept to a minimum, but for every article that was brought in by the hardy men who ventured down the mountain, Ben was willing to pay a hefty price, pulling from the savings he had hidden behind a rock in his chimney.

Ben's thoughts were so tied up with plans for the future he hardly had time to reflect upon his shock at finding out that Thornton McRae's name was at the head of the list of single men who'd expressed a desire to participate in Herman Glover's project. He had tried to bring the subject up with Trap a few times when the two of them were alone in the saloon, but Trap would meander around the matter, usually poking fun at Ben's bachelor status. Trap's favorite comment that riled Ben was, "All of us around here figger you wouldn't be such an ornery old cuss if you'd get yourself a wife." This jab always left Ben a bit speechless because he knew there was a ring of truth to it.

One winter evening, Ben, along with Brother Glover and Widow Simpson, helped the hopeful bridegrooms write letters telling a little about themselves to be sent to Morgan Glover in Boston. A couple of the men even contributed faded photographs of themselves. Ben had to admit that the services of Widow Simpson were highly valuable as the letters were being written. She could make even the most undesirable of the hard-rock miners sound appealing as she coached them on what to write and how to say it. She watched for misspelled words and in some cases even wrote the letters herself for those who had no schooling. Trap, who had little or no formal education, became frustrated quickly at the letter-writing session, which was held in Ben's back room since the Widow Simpson would not set foot in the saloon. He soon threw an old photograph on the table in front of Herman Glover, growling, "Do it yourself! Say whatever you like!" He then stalked into the saloon and helped himself to a shot of whiskey from Ben's shelves.

Ben's spirits were higher than they had been since he had opened the Wet Whistle, and he could almost hear the clink of silver dollars as he dreamed of the imported wives refurbishing their homes at Barnes Emporium and General Store.

He began to get his plans together in a big way after Christmas. This was the slowest time of the year in the mountain mining community. Days were short, and the roads sometimes frozen for days at a time. Often it was impossible to get any ore out of town, so Ben took advantage of the abundance of manpower and the scarcity of regular wages for the working men in order to further his project. For a buck a day, he had his pick of hired help to begin construction of his emporium. At first, the miners guffawed at his plans to begin construction during weather that frequently brought days where the temperature hovered no higher than ten or fifteen degrees and plunged that far below zero through the night. They soon found they had misjudged Ben's determination.

The first morning, Ben had a crew of ten men assembled before dawn. Starting at a point about forty feet from the southwest corner of the Wet Whistle, he directed them to remove all the snow in a large, squarish area to give them room to work. Fortunately, it had not snowed in a few days, so they had to dig through no more than two feet of packed, crusted snow. At the same time, he had another part of the crew build a healthy fire nearby. Using washpots borrowed from several women in town, Ben had snow shoveled in and turned into boiling water within a matter of an hour or so. The men were then told to dump the contents of each washpot slowly onto the frozen ground, one at a time, keeping the circumference as small as possible. Initially, the water froze in puddles, but as more was poured on top little by little, the heat began to penetrate and the first layer of icy glaze melted. Subsequent buckets of boiling water began to make the frozen earth crackle and split; more water poured into the cracks, almost by cupful, began to seep in and thaw it. By midmorning, the men were able to dig a hole far enough into the previously frozen earth to sink a heavy support post three feet into the ground. Into the hole around the post, the men placed small chunks of rock that had been brought in from the surrounding mines.

First there was one layer of stone, then liquid mud poured into the crevices between the rocks, then another layer of stone followed by a generous dump of dry earth to help absorb the moisture and keep the post secure until the mud underneath the surface could become rocklike. The posts were strong enough to support the weight of the structure and stabilize the building.

Ben had been bringing buckets of dirt into his living quarters each night and dumping it into a series of packing boxes to dry, all of which had proved to be an irresistible place for Ben's orange cat. DC made more than a few enemies that day as the men dipped into the dry earth to sift it into the hole around the corner post.

It was almost the end of the day before the first post of the general store was secured. Four more days of the same activity followed, until finally, there were eight heavy-duty posts in place. Then came the massive stones rolled down from the mountainside and placed in three parallel rows to support the flooring beams across the front, back, and middle of the rectangular addition.

The nailing of the rough board walls and chinking the cracks were done with relative ease. Before long, the Emporium had taken enough shape to encourage even the most diligent critics that the venture was beginning to look successful. Ben's ambition began to soar even more with the progress of the building, and he decided to add two small guest rooms over the Emporium to accommodate paying visitors to their town.

He told his brother one day, "Dang, Red, if I keep improving things up here, I might even be able to get a U.S. mail contract for the Emporium to set us up a real postal office!"

Red merely sighed and drained his beer, knowing that if Ben intended to do so, he would probably succeed.

CHAPTER 4

IT WAS WELL into spring before the first letters from the ladies arrived. Dub Cross reined up his big sorrel outside the Wet Whistle and proudly pulled from his saddlebag a packet of mail, mostly pastel-colored envelopes bearing feminine handwriting, tied into a neat bundle and posted by Morgan Glover.

Ben swooped up the package of mail as soon as Dub laid it on the bar. "Spread the word, Dub, that we've got some mail worth noticing tonight, and the first round of drinks will be on me." He knew that Dub, though a married man, would waste little time letting the miners know that a free round was available at the Wet Whistle, and Ben was also sure that the enticing envelopes would pry the price of another two or three rounds out of the men.

It wasn't long after quitting time before the bar was full of men, some clamoring for their first free drink, with a little knot of five men standing together, nervously anticipating the distribution of the letters. Ben shoved a bottle toward them along with glasses, hoping to get them to relax a little before reading their mail.

Even Herman Glover had shown up, although he rarely stepped into a saloon. Ben looked around at the gathering and then approached Brother Glover. He spoke to the preacher in low tones, "Where's Trap? He ain't here!"

Brother Glover tried to respond with a confidence he did not feel, "Oh, I'm sure he'll be along. Let's not wait for him, maybe he worked late." Herman Glover knew that the days at the mine had been pitifully short lately and that

Trap had not always been showing up even when work was scheduled.

There was a letter for each of the men, and Ben drew out the suspense as long as he could while the crowd increased and drank faster. Finally, Ben began to wave the various envelopes in the air, and the men shouted and stomped their feet. All, that is, except the nervous bridegrooms-to-be who still clustered together at the end of the bar. The five had apparently conspired before coming together at the Wet Whistle. As each man's name was read aloud, he reached for his envelope, looked at it briefly, and placed it into a pocket, thus disappointing the onlookers. Hoots and shouts changed to silence as the last of the envelopes was distributed, except for the one addressed to Thornton McRae, which Ben slipped unobtrusively underneath a counter. The five men turned to walk in unison out of the saloon. Henry Henshaw did turn back as they filed through the door to announce apologetically, "We want to read these letters in private. We'll see y'all tomorrow night." Ben motioned to Herman Glover to stay and then tried to build enthusiasm again, shuffling through the remaining mail and reading out each family name, enjoying the looks on the men's faces as they received long-hoped-for mail from their families. He soon found himself growing tired of the hullabaloo after a long day, and he was almost glad when the saloon emptied. When the last man had gone, he turned to Herman Glover, who remained at the end of the bar, sipping coffee.

"What the hell do you suppose became of Trap?" he inquired of the preacher, forgetting his language for a moment.

"Prob'ly just had a long day and was too tired to come in. Give me his letter. I'll get it to him," the preacher said with what he hoped was a reassuring smile.

Ben reached under the counter and withdrew the pale blue envelope addressed to Thornton McRae.

"Oh, Ben, why don't you give me one of them whiskey bottles that's about half full. I'll get your money to you on payday."

"Glover, I didn't think you touched the stuff anymore!"

"It ain't for me, Ben." Although Herman Glover did not drink alcohol, he knew there were times when it had its purposes. He felt that tonight might be one of those times. He had noticed lately that Trap McRae seemed to be withdrawing from the men with whom he worked even more than was usual for a man of his very private nature.

Ben was glad when he was alone. In his quarters, he stripped down to his long johns, stroked the cat briefly, and climbed into bed, leaving the fire to burn itself out. Sleep was elusive, and he lay there thinking of the six miners and almost envying them. He halfway wished there were an eligible woman to court in Elk Fork, and thought briefly of Widow Simpson, then rolled over with a shudder and sought sleep.

Herman Glover rode off at a trot in the direction of Thornton McRae's cabin, troubled by the change he had seen in Trap lately and now tonight's lack of appearance. He had seen Trap angry but stubborn, after he had arrived in town a year and a half past with a badly mangled leg that oozed blood and pus at every step. With determination, Trap had recovered fair use of the leg, although he often cursed when the ankle gave way underneath him and he stumbled. Glover had felt that Trap's spirits had risen after he got a fairly good-paying job at the mine. And Trap had seemed close to becoming a whole man once again when he appeared in church that Sunday morning to declare himself an eligible bridegroom.

Glover was deep in thought when a voice from the shadows startled him.

"Hold up, Glover. What are you doing out here?"

Herman Glover recognized the voice and stopped his

horse. "Trap, step out of the shadows. I was just coming to see you."

Trap stepped out where Glover could see him.

"What are you doin' out here on foot, Trap?"

"Just exercising my ankle. Walkin' and runnin' make it stronger."

There was an awkward silence. The preacher finally filled it in. "I brought you a letter, Trap. I know they told you over at the mine about the letters. The letters that came in from the women."

"Yeah, I guess I forgot," Trap lied thinly. "I'll take the letter and you can get on back home to bed. It's late for you to be out."

"Trap, since your place isn't far, can we go there and talk? Ben sent you a little somethin'." He pulled the half bottle of whiskey from his pocket.

"Let's go." Trap started up the road at a trot.

He invited Glover in from the cold and set out two tin cups beside the bottle that Glover placed on the table.

Glover eyed the cups and the bottle. "I ain't had a drink in maybe five years."

"Well, then it's about time you did." Trap poured a little into each cup.

"You got a little water I can mix with this?" Herman Glover had hesitated, but he knew a man always talked more when he had a drinking companion.

"There's the bucket," Trap said with a nod.

The preacher filled the cup to the rim with water and sat down, sipping slowly. He started off by talking about the mine, letting Trap relax and cool off after his run, which had left him sweaty even on a cold night.

Finally, he confronted Trap with the purpose of his visit. "Why didn't you show up tonight, Trap? You didn't forget."

Trap drained his cup and reached for the bottle again. "I ain't fit to be a marryin' man. I thought I might be since

I give up thoughts 'bout goin' into the mountains again."
He stopped while he poured a small amount into his cup
and went to the water bucket to weaken it.

"What changed your mind?"

"My leg's gettin' better. An' when I saw the snow pourin'
onto those mountains, I knew one day I'd be back up there
or I'd be dead."

"You can do a little trapping and still have a wife here
and a job at the mine when you want it. You've got an obli-
gation to this woman who wrote you this letter. I'll bet
there's even a picture of her in there from the way it feels."

"Well, you take her picture and you marry her."

Glover felt that he might be losing an uphill battle, but
he persisted, although if he had felt the woman would have
him, he would have taken Trap up on his offer. However,
he knew that none of the women had chosen him.

"Why don't you open the letter and just take a look at
the picture."

"I'll open the letter when I please, and if I please."

Glover saw that Trap's cup was half empty, so he poured
a little more from the bottle, bringing the level close to the
rim again.

"Can I open the letter and pull out the picture? I promise I won't read a word—I just want to see her picture."

"Do what you damn please." Trap feigned indifference,
but when Glover pulled out the picture and sat staring at
it for a few minutes with a smile on his face, Trap reached
out and took it from him.

"She's a pretty woman," Glover said, watching Trap's
face for a response.

"Yeah, she is," Trap acquiesced. "But I've nothing for
her."

"You've a nice cabin, one of the best around. It would
make her a good home. You're a good man, make good
money. About as good as any hereabouts. When I wrote

that letter to her for you, I told her you were a trapper part of the year. You bein' gone some won't surprise her."

Herman Glover kept up his persuasion for an hour or more, with the picture of the attractive, dark-haired young woman propped up on the table in front of them. When he left, near midnight, he thought he had Trap McRae convinced that he could be a husband to the woman and maintain his life as a part-time trapper as well; he was certain that McRae's leg would never heal to the point where going into the mountains for long periods would be possible.

Thornton McRae capped the bottle of whiskey, what little was left, and listened with relief as the preacher's horse pounded up the frozen trail. He knew he was between a rock and a hard place and would have agreed to marrying Satan's daughter if it would get the preacher off his back.

Before he blew out the lantern, he took one more look at the picture lying on the table. He went off to bed, knowing there was a lot of time before the women would arrive, if they arrived at all, which he was prone to doubt, having begun to think that no woman in her right mind would travel for weeks to meet a bunch of unshaven miners at Elk Fork. "Even if they try it, they prob'ly won't get here with their scalps," he said to himself as he rolled into his blankets. He promised himself that he would try to read her letter at first light.

CHAPTER 5

THE MOURNFUL WAIL of the train whistle brought Elizabeth Butler out of a sound sleep. For a moment, she was disoriented. The startling sound took her back to her grandmother's house on the outskirts of Boston where she was used to being awakened at four-thirty each morning by the shrill buzzing of the alarm clock. This was when Grandmother Willett had regularly awakened, demanding breakfast and clean linens for her bed. In a sleepy daze, Elizabeth stirred and tried to rise. The firm hand of the passenger in the seat next to her pressed her back down.

"You've been dreamin' again, honey," Mona said.

The husky voice of the woman seated next to her brought Elizabeth back to reality. She sat up and looked around, relieved that she was not in Boston, but in a passenger train headed west. She flexed her legs, which were numb from sitting in a cramped position, and pushed her dark hair back as she leaned toward the window on her right. Daylight was breaking over a horizon of rolling hills, still green but losing the brilliance of early summer. Grays and pinks in the dawning sky suggested another hot and humid day. Memories of the past few days came back to Elizabeth, and she slowly leaned back in her seat.

"I guess you're right, Mona," she addressed to her companion in the aisle seat. Elizabeth put her head back and closed her eyes, trying to sort out dream from reality. What she identified as reality seemed as illusionary as the fantasies that visited her in sleep. A dull headache seemed to pulsate with every rotation of the wheels along the rail. Restlessly, she straightened up and pulled a photograph from her purse and stared at the masculine face that stared back at her.

"Honey, you're gonna wear that picture out, staring at it and fondling it like you do," Mona commented.

Elizabeth felt herself start to blush and thought she must look like a silly, love-struck schoolgirl.

"I know, Mona. But he just seems so unreal. Thornton McRae." She couldn't help but repeat his name as if to give substance to the man.

"Thornton McRae's real, all right. You'll find out how real soon enough." Mona had not needed to be told that although Elizabeth was on the far side of her mid-twenties, she had little experience with men. "I wouldn't put too much stock in that picture though. It looks kind of old and faded to me. Could be he's an old graybeard by now." Then she added, to soften the sharpness of her words, "But he does have nice, kindly lookin' eyes. I'll bet they're brown, or maybe even hazel. I've always been partial to men with hazel eyes."

Mona was a plump redhead with a fondness for blue eye shadow, which was now smeared around the edges of her puffy eyes, swollen after many sleepless hours on a noisy train. She wore a tight-fitting bodice that was cut a trifle too low and was almost the same shade as her eye shadow. Her plump fingers tugged idly at a thin, lacy ruffle around the low neckline of her blouse.

"You still got that headache, Elizabeth?"

Elizabeth nodded.

"Here, take my pillow," Mona commanded and began to stuff it behind Elizabeth's head.

"No, you mustn't. I'm all right." Elizabeth tried to protest, although she knew Mona would not listen. Since the start of their journey from Boston, Mona had pampered Elizabeth, seeing in her an innocence that Mona herself had long since lost even though the two women were about the same age.

Actually, Mona had felt an immediate, inexplicable sense of friendship with the other young woman as soon as the two had met at the train station in Boston. One look at the dark-gray gabardine dress with its high, hand-crocheted collar and the small black hat, its ribbons tied in a bow to one side of Elizabeth's chin, had told her this woman, although not expensively dressed, had the character of a real lady. When the other women were introduced to her, Elizabeth greeted each of them with warm sincerity and a genuine smile. She seemed slightly nervous, and Mona had guessed, correctly, as she found out later, that this was Elizabeth's first trip outside Boston in a long time.

"Well, one more day, and we'll be off this damn train. A stagecoach can't be much worse."

At first Elizabeth had been shocked to hear a woman curse; but Mona's good nature had won her over, and Elizabeth came to accept the coarse language.

The women who traveled in Elizabeth's group numbered seven, including herself; Elizabeth sensed there were seven different stories ranging from desperation and hopelessness to a quest for adventure. Her own story ran the full extent of the range. Six of these women were on their way to the western frontier for the purpose of marriage, marriage to men whom they had yet to meet. The seventh woman was their chaperone, whom Herman Glover had insisted upon to give the traveling ladies the appearance of decorum.

Elizabeth found herself telling Mona her story the first day of the trip.

Elizabeth had been born in a sod house far out on the Kansas plains on a blistering hot day in the middle of summer. Her youthful parents had hoped that the ease of her birth and the health of the newborn was a sign from God that he would end their hardship and bless them with bountiful harvests or at least a decent crop or two that would enable them to provide for their child. Their hope was short-lived. When Baby Elizabeth had seen scarcely more than one week of life, a great storm of locusts darkened the midday sun and descended upon Edward Butler's wheat field. Two days later, the insects had left behind only stubbled land and great cavities in the sod shanty's wooden door where they had gnawed and scraped as if the door too were a living plant.

Having already survived three years of near starvation, Edward and Mary Butler packed up their few belongings and once more headed west, seeking only a place where they might start over once more.

These were the days of the great gold boom in Colorado Territory, and the Butlers ended up making their home in a small town by the name of Creek Junction, where Edward Butler went to work in another man's mine and Mary did washing for many of the single men working nearby. There they lived and flourished for the first ten years of Elizabeth's life.

The memories of the first ten years sustained her through the next seventeen. Her parents had prospered and life had been good. Edward Butler soon had his own modest mine and had built a snug two-room house nearby for his family. Mary no longer had to take in laundry. Elizabeth had always cherished the memories of bright sun-filled days when she and her mother would pan for gold here and there in the streams that converged near Creek Junction and of hunting trips with her father, when they would travel far up into the mountains, bringing back enough food for the family table to carry them through several weeks. She had special memories of the days when she would ride her small pony beside her father, eager for the smell of the pines, the chance to drink coffee out of a tin cup away from her mother's protective eyes, and to sleep on the ground underneath the stars.

Miraculously, long after Mary and Edward Butler had given up hope for another child, a son was born. At nine and a half, Elizabeth doted on the infant, caring conscientiously for both the baby and her mother as Mary slowly recovered.

Her happiness with life at Creek Junction came to an end when Elizabeth was ten years old. Shortly after her birthday, an epidemic of smallpox almost wiped out the town after the disease was introduced by a group of gold-seeking emigrants in a few tattered-topped covered wagons. Mary Butler and baby Frederick had died almost simultaneously; a few days later, Edward followed them. A frightfully ill Elizabeth had been cared for by an elderly neighboring couple who risked the disease to nurse the sick child. Elizabeth awoke from days of high fever and delirium to learn that her family was dead and already buried.

It was then that Elizabeth was sent back to live with her grandmother, Esther Willett, on the outskirts of Boston. Grandma Willett had been frail when Elizabeth arrived, but not too frail to establish herself as a strict disciplinarian. It had been difficult for Elizabeth, a child who had been used to spending most of her days outdoors, running barefoot in summer in loose homemade dresses and trudging in boots behind her father during the winter, dressed in boys' jeans and long underwear. Her life in Boston became tedious days in a dismal schoolroom, long Sundays in the Presbyterian church, nights spent studying under Esther Willett's watchful glare, and worst of all, endless hours at the sewing bees that her grandmother insisted they both attend as long as Grandma Willett was able to hobble down the street with her cane.

It got worse when Grandma Willett had her stroke. Elizabeth was scarcely fifteen when she found herself caring for an invalid, taking food to her, sometimes having to feed her with a spoon, changing the bed linens, and bathing her from a small washbasin. The twelve remaining years of Esther Willett's life made even the old days of the sewing bees seem pleasant.

Though Elizabeth felt a guilty sense of relief when her grandmother passed on, the death also caused her to feel a deep despair. Her grandmother had spent so many years in a life that, to Elizabeth, seemed devoid of pleasure, a life that threatened to swallow her up as it had her grandmother. At twenty-seven, Elizabeth had no real friends, only a few neighbors and close acquaintances from the church who dropped in from time to time, and certainly no male companions. Her life had allowed little opportunity for pleasure. In a way, Elizabeth was happy that this was the case because it would make her leaving easier.

Elizabeth had known since her first day in Boston that she would one day return to the West. She had managed to finish her schooling with good grades and figured this would enable her to support herself teaching in some small school. Over the years, Esther Willett had been forced by illness to hand over the management of the household to Elizabeth, and the young woman had managed steadily to put away a dollar or two now and then so that she would not be left penniless when the old lady passed on. Elizabeth had not known the contents of her grandmother's will, but she was not surprised to learn that Grandma Willett left her home and what money she had to her only surviving son, Charles, with the understanding that Elizabeth receive five hundred dollars and could live out her days with Charles and his wife, Tillie, if no favorable match could be found for her.

It was soon after Esther Willett's death that Elizabeth had seen the advertisement in the local paper. As she related the story to Mona she could not remember the exact wording, but the advertisement had read something like *Honorable Men in the West Seek Respectable Women for Marriage, Morgan Glover, Esquire, Marriage Broker and Attorney at Law.*

Elizabeth had told Mona her story as the train rolled along. When she finally grew silent, Mona asked, "What would have happened if you had not answered the ad?"

"I expect Uncle Charles might have let me live in Grandma's house for a while until they decided that was not suitable, and then they would have made me move in with them. They might have tried to marry me off to some widower twice my age," Elizabeth stared out the train window, and her voice trailed off. "I would've been as dead as Grandma before long. I hated Boston from the first day I saw it!"

Mona had a lot more questions she would have liked to ask, but the finality in Elizabeth's voice kept her quiet.

Mona had been an encouragement to Elizabeth from the start of the trip. Elizabeth had tried to emulate Mona's lighthearted cheerfulness, but the best she could manage was an optimism born of the five hundred dollars her grandmother had seen fit to leave her and the almost one hundred dollars left from her private stash of funds after she had purchased clothing for the present journey. Elizabeth was comforted to know she could buy her transportation to another settlement if Elk Fork and Thornton McRae did not seem suitable. The cash was hidden inside the valise she carried, enclosed in a pink embroidered bag that her grandmother had given her on her sixteenth birthday.

Along with the money were stashed a faded letter that Elizabeth's mother had written to Esther Willett shortly before Mary's death, a small painting of Mary and Edward done at the time of their wedding, and a small leather pouch containing an exquisite cedar carving of a bear with tiny figures of Indian dancers carved around the base on which the bear stood. These were all Elizabeth had with her to remind her of her family.

Mona did not volunteer her own story, and Elizabeth did not ask. Their close proximity in the train's cramped interior gave them plenty of opportunity to scrutinize each other, but the women carefully refrained from asking prying questions, choosing instead to let each reveal about herself whatever she wished. It did not take careful observation for Elizabeth to quickly perceive two divergent natures within the group.

There were two other women, Lydia and Frances, who, like Mona, had the flashy look that Elizabeth had been taught to associate with what her grandmother's Boston associates discreetly called loose women. Their makeup usually was applied too generously, and often, not very carefully. Their dresses were brightly colored and frequently revealed an excess of ankle or bosom. But they were friendly, likable women, somewhere close to Elizabeth's age. Elizabeth, always generous with her judgment of people, felt they were somewhat self-conscious about the clothing they wore, perhaps out of lack of choice. She complimented them on their hairdos, which were simple and almost demure. Like Mona, Lydia and Frances kept themselves meticulously clean. Except for their dress and makeup, Elizabeth could see little about them to criticize except their tendency to be overly friendly with the men they encountered aboard the train or in the train stations.

On the other hand, there were two tiny little women who looked as if they could have been sisters, from the straight lines of their mouths to their severely pulled-back hair. Even their darting eyes were framed by almost identical patterns of wrinkles. Their dresses were plain and their shoes sturdy. Birdie Hollister and Mollie Franklin professed to be widows. Elizabeth guessed their reasons for such a trip might range toward desperation and hopelessness; yet she sensed a strength in the two women and thought they'd be likely to last in the small mining town.

Mona and Elizabeth secretly agreed that the two were undoubtedly spinsters and, in quiet whispers, conspiratorially described the women as they might look if dressed in stylish clothing, with fashionable bonnets and hairstyles. The younger women concluded that Birdie and Mollie, whom they estimated to be in their mid-forties, held some promise of being reasonably attractive.

The seventh woman of their group was Lucinda Barlow, who had introduced herself as their chaperone. Mrs. Barlow hardly acted the part. The well-dressed, heavyset woman with wide streaks of gray through formerly blond hair was frequently engaged in card games here and there throughout the train. She sometimes talked Mona, Lydia, and Frances into a quick game of poker. But if it suited her mood, she likewise engaged the male passengers in card games, seemingly without a flicker of thought as to the impropriety of such an act.

Lucinda Barlow did keep her covey of women cheered up. When any one of them expressed doubt about the steps they were taking or voiced any concern about the future, Mrs. Barlow spoke up with enthusiastic praises for Elk Fork, the prosperity of the little town, and the character of its inhabitants.

"Who would guess she's never seen the place. She sounds like she was one of the founders," Mona quipped sarcastically to Elizabeth in private.

Mona's exuberance almost matched Mrs. Barlow's.

"Elizabeth, these men have a big desire for us. They've put out a lot of money to get us there. So remember, don't settle for less than the maximum you can get out of Thornton McRae. Don't settle for no little two-room cabin. We both want fine houses with maybe four or five rooms. We're young enough to give these gents a lot of kids. Be sure you remind your man of that—tell him sons, that you can give him a lot of sons."

Elizabeth would smile at these remarks and murmur something polite to show she was listening. The more she heard of the excited chatter from her traveling companions, the greater became her doubts that any woman on the train, except perhaps the birdlike spinsters, had entered into this situation with any deep perception as to its real consequences. Birdie and Mollie simply sat quietly through the outpouring of enthusiasm, often knitting some item that they pulled from their valises.

There were a number of moments when Elizabeth considered getting off the train at the next stop and turning back. But there was nothing to return to. She finally found some inner peace when she convinced herself that the best solution was to continue the journey to Elk Fork and meet Thornton McRae. The marriage could be delayed until she felt sure that a future with this stranger was best for her. Her mind thus made up, her spirits brightened considerably.

Finally, the long rail journey ended. It was early morning when the women gathered their things and stepped from the train. They stood together and looked at the towering peaks far to the west, unable to voice the awe they felt at the sight. For once, the entire group was silent.

All that day the two coaches the women boarded jostled and bounced across the plains, moving swiftly and steadily toward the mountains. A tingle of excitement and a little fear made Elizabeth react to the jolting ride with a queasy, light-headed feeling. She tried to focus her thoughts on the mountains and study the pattern of changing light as the day progressed.

That night was the last of their journey and the first since they had left Boston that they could lie down and sleep without the constant motion of the wheels along the rails rattling through their bones. At a small stage station near the base of the mountains, the women each enjoyed a hot, soapy bath and were grateful for the chance to stretch out on the narrow cots provided for them.

CHAPTER 6

THE TOWN OF Elk Fork had been in a frenzy for a week, ever since they had received confirmation that the ladies would be arriving on Saturday. Plans that had been long in the making went into operation. Under Ben's direction the men constructed tables underneath the spruce trees near the church. The ladies spent much time baking and stayed up most of the night before the anticipated arrival, frying chicken and baking hams.

Friday night, after the town had grown quiet, Ben Barnes pulled out his ladder and a bundle of fabric. Working quickly and silently, he cut flaming red streamers and tied them to the posts in front of the newly constructed Barnes Emporium. He set a few fancy lamps and bolts of brightly flowered material in the windows to catch the ladies' eyes. Back inside the saloon, he emptied several bottles of his best whiskey into a large jar, which he carried into his living quarters and stashed behind the bed. Into the prominently labeled bottles, which brought a good price per drink on sight, he poured the contents of plain black-and-white-labeled bottles. Setting the expensive-looking booze in a prominent spot behind the counter, he gave one last look around and went to bed content with his preparations.

Next morning when he arose and went into the saloon, Ben found Trap McRae sitting alone at a table, a half-empty bottle of the best-labeled whiskey in front of him.

"Trap, what are you doing here? You look like you've been here half the night." Ben took in the weary look on Trap's face and noted he was wearing buckskins.

"Naw, Ben, it ain't been much more'n an hour since I found your door unlocked and decided to help myself." He pulled several coins out of his pocket. "Reckon I'll settle up with you now and be on my way." He stood and stuck the half-empty bottle into the side pocket of his jacket.

A movement outside the window caught Ben's eye. He glanced out and saw Trap's big red sorrel tied to the hitch rail and a fully loaded packhorse beside it. He looked back at Trap. "What in the hell do you think you're doing?"

"I'm leavin', Ben."

Ben stared at him in disbelief, "You're leavin'?"

"Yep," Trap strode toward the door.

"What about that lady, that Miss Butler that's coming here to meet you today? You're soon to be a married man."

"I'm already a married man, Ben. Don't know why I let myself be caught up in these shenanigans of yours anyway. All I done was suggest that you get some saloon women in here, and look how I nearly ended up. Don't know what got into me." He had stopped halfway across the floor, but didn't turn to face Ben as he talked.

Ben was aghast. "What do you mean you're a married man? You don't mean that Indian squaw you got."

As Trap walked out the door, he replied, "That's what I mean." He tightened the cinch on his saddle, mounted, and rode away as Ben stared after him.

It didn't take Ben long to get into action after he realized the finality of Trap's words. The pudgy saloon keeper ran up the street to Brother Glover's small cabin. By the time he made the quarter mile, he had trouble announcing the problem to the preacher. Through gasps and pants, he finally made himself understood.

Herman Glover seemed unabashed. "Don't worry, Ben. It's just a case of the bridegroom fidgets. I'll fetch him back."

Ben sat down on the steps to catch his breath and

watched the preacher bring his horse from the shed and throw the saddle on.

Before riding away, Brother Glover turned back to Ben. "I'll be back with Trap. In the meantime, get Widow Simpson or Betsy or somebody to spread the word. The marryin' ceremony will take place as soon as the women step off the stage. It'll be easier for ever'body that way, without wastin' time. Ever'body's ready for a picnic anyway, so we might as well have a weddin' at the same time."

Not knowing what else to do, Ben did as the preacher told him. When the stage rolled in shortly after noon, the entire town was gathered. Herman Glover had arrived not more than an hour before. He had ridden in with Thornton McRae following, a lopsided grin on his face. Ben had seen Trap inebriated often enough to recognize the look. Without a word, Brother Glover half-led Trap into his cabin. Shortly, the two reappeared, Glover in his preachin' suit and Trap somewhat cleaner looking than when he had ridden in minutes before, but still dressed in his buckskins and still grinning. There was a dark swelling to one side of his chin, and his left eye seemed a little puffy, but no one mentioned this.

As the petticoated passengers stepped out of the coaches one by one, Sheriff Red Barnes and Mayor Ben were there to assist them. The crowd was singing heartily, if a little off-key, "Here Comes the Bride." The ladies were ushered toward a small pagoda that had been constructed at Widow Simpson's demand. It was just large enough to accommodate six couples and the minister.

The six women were looking from one another to the happy spectators and then to the six bridegrooms awaiting them at the pagoda. The women's faces displayed an assortment of emotions. Mona, Lydia, and Frances wore big smiles of amusement. Birdie and Mollie both looked timidly resigned. But Elizabeth wore a stiff mask of panic. In fact, she turned back toward the coach before the quick, firm hand of Lucinda Barlow stopped her.

Smiling graciously to the Barnes brothers, Mrs. Barlow requested, "May I have one moment with my ladies, please? We did not anticipate that the marriage service would be so soon." She pulled the women into a small cluster, still holding tightly to Elizabeth's wrist. She forced herself to sound cheerful.

"Girls, what a surprise! These men are so eager to be your husbands they just can't wait for the nuptials to be performed! What could be better! I will arrange with Mayor Barnes for you to have a place to freshen up before you go to your respective homes." She looked from one to another, giving a reassuring pat here, a peck on the cheek there; she left Elizabeth until last, hoping the calmness of her companions would somehow reassure the frightened young woman. When she came to Elizabeth, Mrs. Barlow gently gripped both her shoulders and looked sternly into Elizabeth's dark eyes, now wide with fright.

"Mrs. Barlow, I can't do this! I can't!"

Mrs. Barlow shook her gently, hoping no one would perceive a problem. "You can, Elizabeth, and you will! You are not going to embarrass all of us, to say nothing of the man who paid your way to be here for him today. Think of someone else's feelings besides your own, you selfish thing!" She held Elizabeth's eyes with her fiery stare until the younger woman finally looked down and gave a small nod.

Elizabeth's display had dimmed what little enthusiasm had been felt among the women for this unexpectedly sudden ceremony, but as the crowd still hummed the wedding march, none could bring a protest to her lips.

To dispel the tension created by the confrontation between Mrs. Barlow and Elizabeth, Mona turned to Lydia and whispered just loud enough for the women to hear,

"I've heard of shotgun weddings before, but this is the first time the gun had to be held on the bride!"

In the meantime, Brother Herman Glover was mopping his brow with a grayed handkerchief. He stole a look at the bridegrooms, particularly Thornton McRae; he caught the eye of each man and gave a reassuring smile. This marriage endeavor had chiefly been Glover's idea, a way to bring respectability into the lives of this small flock of his, and he was determined to see it successfully carried out. He had been painfully disappointed to learn that no bride had been found for him. In spite of his best efforts, Morgan Glover had been unable to find a woman of suitable reputation who would accept a marriage to the backwoods preacher.

Soon the women moved again toward the pagoda, each trying to smile, but each feeling tremulous if not downright scared.

Herman Glover called out the names of each woman and each man as they had been paired by mutual agreement. As he called each name, a man or a woman stepped forth to meet the soon-to-be spouse. "Lydia Williams and Hank Garth. Birdie Hollister and Bill Hatfield. Mona Smith and Haygood Pierce. Mollie Franklin and Elmer Osgood. Frances Thomas and Henry Henshaw. Elizabeth Butler and Thornton McRae." The twelve seemed almost frozen as the minister intoned, "Do you men take as your wives . . ."

The ceremony was over quickly. Tactfully, Brother Glover did not end with the traditional kiss exchanged by bride and groom.

Few words were exchanged between the brides and the grooms for the duration of the festivities. Each sex seemed as shy as the other and welcomed the banter of the congratulatory crowd. Even Mona, Lydia, and Frances were uncharacteristically subdued. The couples stood self-consciously side-by-side, sipping punch and eating from the plates piled high with food, served to them by the ladies of

Elk Fork. Through the afternoon, Betsy Barnes took the women, one or two at a time, to her house to touch up their hair, wash the dust off in a basin of warm water, and change into fresh clothing.

When the afternoon event began to draw to a close, the women hugged each other and spoke reassuring words before each left with her new husband.

Elizabeth and Thornton McRae rode out of town on an aged buckboard provided by Ben Barnes. It was pulled by the unmatched combination of Trap's big sorrel and the packhorse with which he had ridden into town early that morning. Trap's packs were unobtrusively stashed underneath a tarpaulin along with some provisions he had purchased from Barnes Emporium.

Elizabeth's heart was pounding with nervousness, and she feared Thornton McRae might hear it. During the five-mile trip, she tried to cover the sound of it with agitated chatter, hoping she was making sense as she spoke. Trap was polite and responded to her questions, but initiated no conversation on his own.

Finally, they turned from the road onto a small lane barely wide enough for the buckboard. Elizabeth pulled her shawl more closely around her shoulders as tall, thick trees cut off what was left of the sun disappearing over the mountains.

Trap began to grow more talkative as they neared his cabin. "Got this place a few years ago from an old miner and his wife. They had decided to get back to their kids in Kentucky while they were still able to travel. I used to spend most of my time in the mountains, doin' a little prospectin', trappin', and such, but decided I needed a home base."

The small cabin was well-situated among the trees, where it would be sheltered from the cold winter winds, but in a small clearing where it could catch much of the day's sun. It had a small front porch, and a sturdy stone chimney stood on the north. Elizabeth could see it consisted of two rooms.

McRae shoved the front door open and placed her trunk and valise inside. He opened the window shutter to let in the last of the afternoon light. Then he stood there awkwardly as if wondering what to do next.

Elizabeth looked around the room, recognizing its possibilities. "Mr. McRae, you have a nice place here." She addressed him formally, as the ladies in Boston addressed their husbands. "Some of the stories we heard coming out, well, they led me to expect the worst." She stopped short of saying more, not wishing to hurt his feelings.

"Yes, ma'am. I'll just go get the supplies and see to the horses while you get settled." He started for the door, then stopped, looking at the floor quietly. "Then I'll bed down outside on the porch. Just holler if you need anything."

Elizabeth was speechless with relief.

She quickly surveyed the simple interior, almost feeling the spirit of the woman for whom the place had been built. The kitchen occupied most of the main room. There was a large fireplace designed for cooking. Pegs had been placed between the stones framing it when the fireplace was constructed to provide storage for pots and pans and other cooking utensils, although there were few in place there now. A large blackened coffeepot sat on the hearth. A small cupboard was built in the corner to the right, consisting of a rough counter, perhaps two feet wide and three feet long, with a double layer of shelving underneath. The cupboard door stood open, and Elizabeth knelt to survey the contents. Little was there, a can half full of lard, a sack that contained maybe a half pound of flour, a handful of knives and forks, four tin plates, and a chunk of lye soap. Stuck in the far corner was a handful of rags. She was thankful for the supplies that were in the wagon.

The kitchen table was sturdy, with a smoothly sanded top and heavy benches on either side. Across the room were a couch and two chairs built of pine. Each piece had thin cushions covered by a cotton fabric with a small faded print. The room had two small windows, one behind the wooden couch, facing south, the other beside the door, which opened to the west. Each had heavy wooden shutters.

Elizabeth moved on to the bedroom. Here the furnishings were just as sparse, a bed, a night table on which sat a lantern, and a small wardrobe in the corner with one door hanging crooked. Next to that was a small window, heavily shuttered like the others. A mirror with a zigzag crack hung over the night table. The bed was covered by two rough woolen blankets. When Elizabeth pulled them to one side, they appeared to be clean, but there were no sheets, just the mattress ticking of coarse, striped cotton.

Elizabeth felt a flash of despair and glanced around the room quickly to see if there could be some place where sheets might be stored. In dismay, she plopped down on the bed, hardly noticing that it felt soft and comfortable. She forced herself to recall Lucinda Barlow's cheerfulness when she cautioned the women to expect to find crude living conditions. At least, she thought, the blankets were clean, the cabin could be made quite pleasant, and Thornton McRae was polite, if not talkative. While she sat and reflected on the situation, she heard Trap bringing in the supplies and placing them on the kitchen table.

Carrying the lantern into the kitchen, she looked for matches and found a few beside the fireplace. The light from the lantern gave a warm glow to the room when she placed it on the kitchen table. The supplies Trap had brought in were barely ample: flour, beans, potatoes, two large loaves of bread, coffee, and a slab of bacon. Finding herself grateful for small blessings, she put the food away.

That done, she pulled the embroidered bag out of her valise and fingered the portrait of her mother and father, wondering what their opinion would be of the bold action

Elizabeth had taken to escape Boston. Somehow, she felt they would approve. Placing her most valued items, including the money, back inside the bag, she shoved it deeply into the pocket of a new winter coat she had purchased in Boston. She dragged the trunk into the bedroom and hung her clothes in the wardrobe, carefully shaking out the wrinkles and wondering briefly if Thornton McRae had moved his clothing to another storage place, perhaps the shed she had noticed out back as they rode in. When the trunk was empty, she folded the coat and placed it, along with a new pair of boots, inside. So busy had she been with her thoughts that she did not realize Trap had come inside until she heard him rap his knuckles at the bedroom door to get her attention. The sound startled her.

"Ma'am, I didn't mean to scare you. I just thought I would ask if you needed anything before I go to sleep. There's a fresh bucket of water on the table."

She shook her head, "No, everything is fine. Thank you for asking."

After he left her alone, Elizabeth realized she was exceedingly tired. She got into her nightgown, blew out the lantern, slipped between the rough blankets, and ended her wedding day alone and glad of it.

CHAPTER 7

ELIZABETH WAS RELIEVED the next morning when she found that Thornton McRae was gone when she arose. Since it was Sunday, she had not thought that he would be going to the mine, but apparently he had. In the kitchen, a low fire burned in the fireplace, and a pot of coffee was set to one side where it would stay warm. Elizabeth felt a little guilty that she had overslept and had not been up to make breakfast, but glad that she had not had to make conversation with the short-spoken man who was her husband. From the smell of the room, she knew Thornton had fried bacon for breakfast. The aroma enticed her to do the same. Although Elizabeth had never cooked on a fireplace before, she found this one had been designed with flat stones in just the right places for frying, simmering, and warming. She fried the bacon and cut a slice of bread, surprised that she was so hungry after the feast in Elk Fork the prior afternoon.

Breakfast finished, Elizabeth slipped into a pair of comfortable shoes and stepped outside. The morning sun was filtering through the trees like a silver mist. She began to explore her surroundings, going first to the small shed she had noticed the previous afternoon. It obviously housed the horses and what other paraphernalia Thornton accumulated. The big sorrel was gone, and the smaller horse was picketed outside in a patch of thick grass. Inside the shed, there was a little hay, pieces of harness and bridles hanging on pegs, and odds and ends of hardware. An ancient broom leaned in the corner next to what seemed to be a small storage room at the rear. A padlock was on the door, but Elizabeth tried to peer between the cracks around the sides. The interior was dark, and she could see nothing.

Elizabeth approached the woods rather timidly. The trees were tall, with a changing pattern of light pouring through in some places or merely peeping through in others. This was far different from the skimpy forest she had explored on Uncle Charles's farm. She remembered years past when she had prowled through the trees with her father or mother.

Soon she heard the stream, water pushing past rocks with its distinctive sound. As she approached it, she wished for a line to cast into the water, remembering the exhilaration of taking home a flopping trout for the family dinner.

Elizabeth sat down on a smooth stone beside the creek to ponder her situation. Her living arrangements were better than she had expected. She knew in time she would come to love this place. Thornton McRae was another angle to the story. He was not bad-looking, although he had large hairy hands—Elizabeth had always been repulsed by hairy men, but he seemed to be a gentleman. Elizabeth could not imagine ever coming to love him. However, all she had let herself hope for was a man with whom she could live in peace and harmony. Even that looked somewhat questionable now, although she had no experience with men on which to base her judgment. But something seemed to tell her McRae resented her presence. Yet she was glad she had taken the bold step that placed her where she was now.

The house was dusted and swept and the bedding was airing when Betsy Barnes rode up in the middle of the afternoon. Elizabeth was grateful for the visit and even more appreciative of the jars of Betsy's homemade wild plum preserves.

The two sat on the edge of the porch and talked. Betsy filled in many of the gaps in Elizabeth's knowledge of the people of Elk Fork, particularly the men who had married her traveling companions. Betsy told the good things she could recall and avoided the issue when she couldn't find something good to say. Elizabeth likewise spoke of the positive attributes of Thornton McRae and kept silent about the peculiarities of their relationship. She did venture a question.

"Tell me, Betsy, is Thornton McRae an unusually shy person? He doesn't seem to talk much."

Betsy laughed and explained as much about Trap's background as she could discreetly: "Thornton McRae—most of us call him Trap—has spent most of his years in the mountains, doing some trapping, some prospecting. Trapping has all but died out the last few years, and we've been hoping that he would stick around here and get on with a regular life. With this marriage, it looks like we're going to get our wish. He's never been one to spend much time around people, except for the past year or so since he had that accident that nearly cost him his leg. We were all very happy when he decided to get married. Give him time, Elizabeth. Trap's a good man, and I'm sure it will work out. You know, he was the first man to commit himself with the marriage proposal that Brother Glover suggested. The other men sort of followed his example—I guess they thought if Trap McRae was going to settle down to family life, maybe it was time for them to do the same."

This explanation lifted Elizabeth's spirits, and she went on to ask Betsy's opinion on another matter.

"Do you think Mr. McRae would allow me to ride that horse?" She motioned toward the pack animal picketed nearby.

"That horse? Believe me, you don't want to try to ride that animal! He's a strange one. Nobody around here has been able to saddlebreak that varmint. Now, he'll carry a pack or pull a wagon and be gentle as a dog. But try getting close to him with a saddle and he goes plumb crazy."

Elizabeth was disappointed. "Betsy, I must have some

way of getting around. It would mean I could go to town and visit or go to church, do my shopping, things I don't expect Mr. McRae to have much enthusiasm for. I have a little money that my grandmother left me. Maybe I'll ask Mr. McRae to use it to buy a horse for me!"

Betsy could see from the tone of her voice and the way her eyes lit up that this was important to Elizabeth. Betsy paused before she spoke and chose her words carefully.

"Elizabeth, I am sure you are aware of your husband's pride and independence. He values those qualities in himself, but I cannot see that he would value those same qualities in his wife."

Elizabeth looked puzzled, and Betsy could see that she needed to explain further. "I doubt that he would want you riding into town regularly, even to church. He is a very private person, and I imagine he thinks you, as his wife, will follow his example. And I'm afraid it would hurt his pride for his wife to purchase her own animal." Betsy was silent for a moment, studying the disappointment on Elizabeth's face.

"Elizabeth," she spoke softly and studiously. "This may be poor advice, but if it means that much to you, then do it and tell him about it after you have the bill of sale in your name and in your hands. After you think it over, if that is what you decide to do, I'll help you find a good horse. I have a couple in mind that you could possibly buy for a reasonable price."

Elizabeth turned quiet, and Betsy respected her silence. Betsy's explanation did not satisfy Elizabeth, even though she did not question the accuracy of it. It just didn't add up; Thornton McRae's indifference, the cold civility he showed toward her, and now the idea that he would expect that she stay isolated on this property day after day. She had spent too many years of her youth confined to her grandmother's house due to the old woman's illness to tolerate a similar confinement. Before Betsy left, Elizabeth accepted her offer of assistance and gave her the money with which to purchase a horse and saddle.

Elizabeth had Trap's meal prepared when he rode in that night. She met him at the door with a quiet greeting as he was dousing his face at the washbasin that sat just outside. He grunted a short acknowledgment. Rubbing his hands on a ragged towel that hung nearby, he nodded toward two squirrels lying on the step. "Any chance you know how to clean a squirrel?"

"No, I'm afraid I don't."

"Didn't think you would. Heat the fryin' pan, then, while I get the squirrels ready."

"But supper is already done."

McRae hung his head in exasperation. "For tomorrow. Cook 'em tonight so we can eat 'em tomorrow. Gotta have something to take to the mine in the mornin'. Ain't no fancy cafe like you may be used to."

Elizabeth felt her face burning with embarrassment. He was right, of course. She had not thought to plan for his midday meal and felt a sharp stab of guilt at her omission. Then she thought in self-defense, he hasn't left me a lot of groceries here to plan with.

Trap McRae fell asleep that night long after the moon had disappeared, and he felt frustrated and torn. He admitted to himself that slender Elizabeth was an unusually attractive woman, with her shiny brown hair and deep, dark eyes. No doubt she was a good, decent woman who would cook his meals and keep his house clean. In fact, it was this latter thought that somehow bothered him the most. He couldn't figure out why his temper had flared so when he walked into the freshly cleaned house. Trap was not a man given to much analysis of himself, but he knew that the urge to ride out for good had never been stronger than when he saw that Elizabeth had cleaned the cabin while he was gone and had even spread the blankets over some juniper bushes to air. He figured the next thing she would do was to send him down to the stream with a chunk of lye soap.

Trap had tried to blame Ben Barnes for getting him into this situation, and from time to time, he felt an urge to curse Herman Glover for forcing him back to town when he had come so close to escaping this commitment. He had avoided so much, so often, by simply riding away. Eventually, however, in a roundabout way, Trap came to face the truth that he himself was to blame. Many months ago, when he knew the mountain passes would soon be closed by deep snowdrifts, Blue Flower and his Indian family had seemed so far away. His injuries at the hands of the Arapaho had made him doubtful that he would ever be able to resume the free mountain life. He knew the beaver and other game were practically gone. Loneliness and a sense of resignation had made the idea of a white woman to care for his needs seem awfully inviting.

The coming of spring had begun to change all that and bring out the instincts that survived in his spirit. The rivers and streams swollen with runoff from the high peaks had told him the passes would soon be open. He no longer walked with much of a limp, and he began to test his endurance by walking as far as he could each day when the work in the mine was done. By summer, he was able to walk many miles through the dark mountains, sleep a couple of hours, then return in the morning fit for another hard day.

He knew he was physically able to return to the mountains. He began to argue with himself, to tell himself that he had made a commitment and had obligations, and he was left with a growing bitterness. He longed to see Blue Flower and his son, to be with the growing boy to teach him some of the white man's ways to complement Blue Flower's teachings and the strength and wisdom the boy would acquire from the Utes.

CHAPTER 8

AFTER HER FIRST day's embarrassment at having overslept and neglected Trap's breakfast and midday meal, Elizabeth vowed it would happen no more. She began to sleep fitfully through the night, awaking often and peering out through the small window near her bed. She had a small clock that had been her grandmother's, but the alarm had broken, and the time couldn't be read without lighting the lantern. Elizabeth began to learn the fundamental use of the stars and the moon.

Meal planning and preparation were difficult because of the limited variety of supplies. It was a special treat when Trap rode in one afternoon with a large can of fresh milk and a flour sack containing eight large eggs precariously tied to his saddle. Elizabeth's eyes lit up with delight when she learned what he'd brought.

"Where did you get this?"

"Ole Joe Sipes lives out close to the mines. He keeps a few milk cows and chickens, sells the stuff to the miners now 'n then. I guess you know what to do with this stuff better than you did with a couple of squirrels." It was his first attempt to tease her.

Elizabeth looked at him sharply to see if there was any sign of mockery. Detecting none, Elizabeth replied graciously, "I do indeed."

From then on, Trap regularly brought home milk and eggs, and she regularly searched the woods for berries to use for a pie or cobbler, though few were ripening, since the frequent afternoon thunderstorms passed without depositing any rain.

Their diet improved, but not their relationship. Elizabeth would stare at herself in the cracked mirror, wondering what she was doing wrong. She bathed frequently in the stream and splashed herself with cologne each evening before Trap arrived home. She brushed her hair until it shone and then she'd tie ribbons in it. It was still a relief to her that Trap slept on the porch, but she would have welcomed a look or word of approval directed at something besides her cooking.

Thoughts of what was happening in town came to bear on her mind, and she wondered how Mona and her other traveling companions had fared. When Sunday came, Trap left for the mine and she read her Bible alone, longing to be in church. A thought crept into her mind and grew: perhaps she could walk into town. The thought would not leave, and days later, she set out as soon as Trap had left for work.

She had judged that it was about five miles into town, the longest distance Elizabeth had ever walked. The morning was brisk and cool, and the first hour went by quickly. The second was somewhat slower, even after she sat and rested in the shade of a pine for several minutes. But her exhaustion was forgotten as she approached town. She fingered the coins in her skirt pocket and was drawn to Ben's Emporium. It had been a long time since she had been able to browse through a store.

When she entered, Ben was stooped over a barrel, but he looked up when he heard the door open. Seeing who it was, he lifted his hand as if to smooth down a shock of nonexistent hair.

"Well, I'll be, it's Missus McRae."

"Mr. Barnes, how nice to see you again."

"Is there something I can help you with, ma'am?"

"I'd just like to look around. It's been a long while since I've been in a store, especially one as nice as this." She was surprised at the stock of goods he had. "If you don't mind,

I'll just browse a little. All I really need to buy is a sack of sugar, but I'd like to look."

"Look all you want, ma'am. It's good to see you again." He retreated out of sight, but kept stealing glances at the attractive young woman as unobtrusively as he could while she examined all the merchandise.

He could see that the dress goods and the bedding caught her eye, and he hoped she would make a selection, but she didn't.

Elizabeth fingered the coins in her pocket again, wanting to make a purchase, but she did not want Trap to know she had been to town. She thought she could pass off the sugar as a gift from Betsy if he even figured out that she had it; with a sigh, she passed everything up and went to the counter to pay for her sugar.

Ben, in the meantime, had been wondering how he could prolong his contact with this pretty female. He suddenly had an idea, "Miz McRae, have you noticed any mice around your place?"

"Mice, heavens no!" She shuddered a little. "I can't stand mice. Why do you ask?"

"Well, come fall, you'll likely have a bunch of 'em. The field mice'll move in like an army to escape the cold. What you'll need is a cat."

"A cat? No, I don't think Mr. McRae would want a cat around."

"He'll thank you a million times over if there's no mice to eat his horse feed. Just happens there's a litter of kittens over at Betsy's. DC here is the daddy. Why don't we go take a look? You don't have to say yes yet. They're brand new babies still."

"I don't think we want a cat, Mr. Barnes, but my next stop was going to be at Betsy's anyway. I'll take a look while I'm there."

"If you're goin' that way now, I'll walk with you if you've no objections."

"I would be glad for the company."

Betsy was in the middle of entertaining her sewing circle when they arrived. The moment she threw the door open and Ben could see the women inside, he began to back away with an excuse that he should get back to the store.

Betsy did not let him get away with it: "Nonsense, Ben, if anybody needs your services at the store, let them wait. Let's sample a little bit of this chocolate cake that's out in the kitchen, waiting for us. Besides, Elizabeth's friend, Mona Pierce, is here."

This seemed to convince Ben to brave the crowd of women.

Mona appeared behind Betsy as Elizabeth and Ben entered. She came forward quickly, holding out both her hands.

Elizabeth was more interested in news about Mona's new life and that of their other traveling companions than in seeing the kittens. After a few moments of conversation with the other ladies present, Elizabeth and Mona followed Ben to the back porch where the kittens squirmed in a box. Ben hovered over the two women and the nest of squirming, mewing kittens, praising the little animals as if next week's food depended upon his sales job. Gruff though he might be with DC, Ben could hardly stand the thought of DC's offspring going without decent homes.

Finally, Elizabeth fell prey to the kittens' charm and Ben's persuasion. "You're right, Mr. Barnes. I probably should have a cat. I'll take one when they're weaned." Ben was greatly pleased when she selected a little orange male that looked as if he would become the image of DC. After that, Ben accepted a piece of chocolate cake Betsy had placed on a saucer for him and headed back to the store. As he left, he turned back to Mona, "Don't forget to tell Missus McRae about our business deal."

Elizabeth looked at her with a puzzled expression. "A business deal with Mr. Barnes?"

"I'll get to that later. Let's talk about you. Honey, you look tired. Have you been gettin' enough sleep?" she asked mischievously.

"Mona, I wish I knew more about men. Mr. McRae seems awfully, well, awfully standoffish. Is that normal?"

"Standoffish?" Mona queried, trying to figure out just what Elizabeth meant by the word. Not quite sure about her friend's meaning and just as unsure as to how to inquire further, Mona rushed to comfort Elizabeth as best she could.

"Well, honey, Mr. McRae's been a bachelor all his life, as I hear, and you've never had any experience with men. I'm sure it'll take time for the two of you to get used to each other. Just be patient. You're pretty as a picture, and I'm sure your man knows how lucky he is to have a woman like you."

Eager to change the subject, Mona rushed on, "Now you take my Haygood—he's had him one wife and she died several years ago. But I have to give the first Mrs. Pierce her credit. She made him into a first-class husband."

Elizabeth's spirits picked up as Mona described her good fortune in marriage.

"And, Elizabeth, I'm going to go to work for Ben Barnes!" she exclaimed happily.

"You'll be clerking at the Emporium? That is wonderful! He has such a nice place."

"No, silly, it's much more fun than that. I'll be singing and playing the piano at the Wet Whistle. The piano just got here last week!"

Elizabeth was almost speechless. "You'll be performing in a saloon? Mr. Pierce is going to allow you to do that?"

"Oh, it'll just be on Saturday nights, and Haygood says it'll give him a chance to be out with the boys without him gettin' in trouble with the wife. We both think it'll be great fun!"

"I didn't know you were talented, Mona."

"I don't know how talented I am, but I've sung a song or two at church, and these people around here are pretty desperate for entertainment. Lydia and Frances think it's a good idea, and they've both promised to come in once a month or so to hear me. I ain't sure what Birdie and Mollie think; the whole idea prob'ly set their tongues to clickin' like knittin' needles. But what the heck! With the extra money, I can put up some curtains and maybe buy a new bedspread.

"Of course," she continued, "they prob'ly won't be lettin' me sing at church no more. May not let me in the door." She giggled.

Betsy insisted that Elizabeth stay for lunch with the women, promising to deliver her home in plenty of time for her to have supper ready when her husband got home.

When Elizabeth and Betsy rode out of town that afternoon, Betsy said, "Elizabeth, I've been dragging my feet about acquiring a horse for you. I wasn't sure but what you'd change your mind after a while. I can see now that you're pretty serious if you walked five miles into town. I promise to see you again soon and bring a horse to you."

"Betsy, I want to ask you what you think about Mona singing and playing the piano in the saloon. In Boston, it would be a disgrace for a woman to do such a thing."

"Well, the Wet Whistle isn't just any saloon, Elizabeth. We don't have strangers coming through wanting to take advantage of women who might be performing there. Naturally, some of the women around here are going to think the worst of Mona for doing it. She may not even be invited to the sewing circle get-togethers when they're held at anyone's house but mine. But I see no harm in it if it's agreeable with her and Mr. Pierce." Betsy started to tell Elizabeth about the progression of events that had led from the proposal to have saloon women in the Wet Whistle to the negotiations for marriageable women, then thought better of it and held her tongue.

Betsy continued in a slightly different vein, "However, Elizabeth, if you don't mind some advice from me, let me say that I think it would be a good idea if you told Trap about Mona's new business dealings with Ben Barnes. You can tell him I told you the story if you don't want him to know about your visit to town. It might make your desire for a horse to ride to church seem tame in comparison."

The next morning at breakfast Trap accepted Elizabeth's comments about the visit from Betsy without a response until she got to the part about Mona's new job at the Wet Whistle. Then he said between bites, "I knew she was no good the minute I saw her. Pierce would be smart if he put her on a fast horse, headed it toward the east, and hit it with a red-hot poker."

Elizabeth could not choke back her anger. "Thornton McRae, I'll have you know that Mona Pierce is one of the kindest, gentlest people I have ever met. She would do anything in the world for a friend."

Before she could get further, Trap snapped, "A woman like that ain't got no friends, and I'd better never hear of you havin' anything to do with her."

Elizabeth grabbed the water bucket and set out at a fast pace toward the stream.

CHAPTER 9

IT WAS ONLY a matter of days until Betsy rode in about mid-morning, leading a mare. Elizabeth was doing laundry when she heard the horses approaching. When Betsy and the horses appeared, she rushed toward them, drying her hands on her apron.

"She's beautiful! Simply beautiful!"

Indeed, the horse was a beauty—mostly a creamy white, with dark reddish-brown coloring around her neck and hindquarters. Elizabeth could see that it was a well-bred animal.

"Betsy, I can't afford a horse like this! What would she cost?" Elizabeth stopped short, bracing herself for disappointment.

Betsy was pleased to see the look of admiration on Elizabeth's face.

"She's paid for already, and I brought some of your money back. Millie belonged to Emma Peterson, who passed on a couple of months ago. Emma loved this horse like it was a child. Since Emma's been gone, it's been a sad reminder to Mr. Peterson. When I told him about you, he knew you would love Millie and said he felt she should belong to you. So we got her for half what she's worth."

Betsy had been able to get a good, though somewhat worn, saddle for practically nothing, so now she gave fifty dollars back to Elizabeth.

"Congratulations! Hop on, let's go for a ride. Millie wants to get to know you."

Elizabeth had not been on a horse in several years, not since her grandmother's health prevented her visits to her uncle's farm. Now her fondness for the creatures came rushing back. Seeming to sense her affection, the horse nuzzled her warmly.

Before Trap was due home from the mine, Elizabeth led the horse a short distance from the cabin, where she could not be seen. Then she went back to finish supper and to prepare herself for breaking the news about the horse. Nothing had changed over the last few days to indicate that a better relationship was developing between the two of them.

After Trap had arrived and washed his hands, he came in and sat at the table.

"Prints outside. Who was here today?"

"Betsy was here for a while."

"Who else? There was two horses."

"Well, yes, there was another horse. Let me tell you about her."

She tried her best to explain why the horse was important to her. Although she had written about her past to him before coming west, Elizabeth had never discussed the death of her parents, her childhood, and the confinement of those long years, caring for her grandmother. She explained how those years had made her promise herself that she would never endure such restraint again. She appealed to him to understand and tried to compare her having the mare to his feelings of freedom in the mountains. With mention of his trapping days, his face began to harden and his jaw clenched as his chewing slowed.

Finally he said between bites, "Well, go bring the horse to the shed. Can't leave her there for grizzlies."

When she got back with the horse, Trap was outside to help stable Millie. He looked the animal over and said, "Good mare. You did all right for yourself."

Nothing else was said about the matter.

The next day Elizabeth returned from a short ride around mid-morning. As soon as she rode in, she knew something was wrong. The packhorse, usually picketed or hobbled outside, was not there.

Horse thieves! she thought to herself as she pulled Millie up shortly, her eyes darting here and there, expecting to see intruders. She turned Millie quietly back into the trees, where she waited breathlessly for some moments. Seeing and hearing nothing, she slid off the horse and made her way cautiously to the cabin door. Quietly, she pushed the door open and looked around. Nothing seemed to have been disturbed; then she noticed that McRae's bedroll, which she had set inside before she left, was missing. She ran outside to the shed. The storage-area door was standing open. Peering in, she saw that it was almost empty. She backed outside, trying to sort out her thoughts. Should she ride for Sheriff Barnes? Something held her back.

The realization struck: Trap McRae had left her! She knew that somewhere in the back of her consciousness she had expected this. Many times she had considered leaving him, but she had no place to go. Thornton McRae did— the mountains. She looked through a latticework of branches toward the highest peak she could see in the distance as if she might pick him out on the far slopes.

The tears of frustration that she had held back over the last several days finally came with a rush. She sat down on a stump and sobbed heavily, wiping her eyes on the hem of her dress. The sobs stopped and still she sat there, staring at the ground until she heard a low snort behind her and felt a nudge underneath her left shoulder.

"Hello, Millie." She responded by turning and cupping the soft nose to her face. "Let's go for water." Getting the bucket from the porch, she headed for the stream, Millie following. After the bucket was filled, she sat down on a stone and watched the waters flow by while the horse drank.

Presently, she came to the conclusion that maybe things were not as bad as they seemed. After all, she had a secure shelter, a good horse, ample food for a while, and some money. This place already felt like home, with or without Thornton McRae—probably a little more so without his petulant silence every night.

"Come, Millie, let's go home."

Elizabeth was more than a little ashamed that her husband had left her. She lay awake most of the night, wondering what people would think of her that she could not keep a husband even a month. If only there was some way to keep them from knowing, but soon it would get around at the mine that Thornton McRae had not shown up for work and people would be asking questions.

By morning, she had a plan that might work, at least for a while. After breakfast, she rode into town.

"Good morning, Mrs. McRae," Ben said as she walked into the Emporium.

"Good morning, Mr. Barnes. I wonder if I might ask you for a favor." She rushed on not waiting for his answer. "Mr. McRae would like you to get a message to his employer. It seems Mr. McRae has decided to be out of town for a while, said he wants to do a little prospecting on his own." She wondered if her story sounded plausible when Ben looked at her with obvious surprise on his face.

"Oh, he has? Well, Mrs. McRae, I think that is right good news. Trap never did take much to bein' in that dark hole all day. Me, I've been afraid he'd take to trappin' again, and that ain't no decent life for a man, especially with the mountains bein' nearly trapped out. Maybe this will take his mind off, well, off things," he finished hurriedly. "In the meantime, if there's anything me or my brother can do for you, let us know." He wondered to himself how a man in his right mind could leave such an attractive and pleasant woman to go off poking around on the mountainside.

"I did come to purchase a few items, Mr. Barnes. Sheets. I need some bedsheets."

Purchases made, Elizabeth called on Betsy Barnes and Mona, spreading her story with a smile. She rode out of town, glad that she had found her friends happy—and relieved that her story had apparently been accepted.

On the morning of his departure, Thornton McRae had set out for the mine as usual, but he was burdened with feelings of guilt. He had slept little the night before; when sleep did come, dreams of Blue Flower and Thorn Dove, his son, tormented him. When he awoke alone on the cold porch, he thought of the woman inside the cabin, and yet he knew he could not go in to her. During the last year, he had done his best to put his past behind him, to become a white man again, and he had thought a white woman would be the key to his efforts.

Thornton McRae was basically a practical man and knew the time was coming when it would be impossible for the white man to live among the Indians. Already the streams were just about trapped out, game was becoming scarce, and white settlers were pressing in upon the Indian lands in ever-increasing numbers. As conflicts arose more frequently, the outcome was growing clearer to him. If Blue Flower's people were forced onto reservations, like so many tribes, what would become of her? He knew it would be better for Blue Flower to have a husband of her own people to stand by her and the child. A white man would be cast from the tribe by the white soldiers, leaving the woman alone at the time of greatest crisis.

Now Trap pondered his duty to both women. He should stay away from Blue Flower for her own benefit. He should stay with Elizabeth and be her husband, providing a traditional life for her in the white man's world.

Ultimately, on this morning of anguish and indecision, Trap succumbed to the lure of the wilderness and the harmony of his life with Blue Flower. He knew Elizabeth's looks and the scarcity of women would assure her of a man in no time, and he had no regard for the legalities of marriage vows.

So he left for work as usual that morning and then returned to the cabin, hiding out in the woods, confident that Elizabeth would take her newly purchased horse for a ride before the day's end. He waited until she rode out, then he rode in. He hastily strapped his gear on the packhorse. At the last minute, he remembered the fine wool coat that Elizabeth had brought with her. On an impulse, he went inside and took it from the trunk where he had watched her place it. Knowing how delighted Blue Flower would be with the garment, he left in its place a twenty-dollar gold piece and a hastily written note.

Then Trap turned his horses up into the hills and sequestered himself among the trees for many days, putting a sense of peace back into his life.

CHAPTER 10

IN THE SHED, Elizabeth found a couple of battered pans, which she recognized as vessels used for panning gold. Whenever the weather was good enough, she took these to the creek and scooped up sediment from the streambed, swirling the contents as she remembered her mother doing and looking for tiny gold flecks. Her hopes of finding anything were scant, but the activity eased her mind when concerns about the future began to torment her.

Late one morning as she waded in the edge of the creek, the crunch of a footstep on a nearby rotten log caused her to look up sharply. A stranger stood frighteningly close, watching her from across a fallen log. Straightening quickly, she dumped the muddy contents of the pan down the front of her skirt.

"You startled me!" she declared with relief when she realized it was a young white man, not much more than a boy.

"I didn't mean to skeer you, ma'am. Do you mind if I get a sip of water? These woods is hot today." After drinking several times from his cupped hands, he retreated to the fallen log, where he seated himself.

"Who might you be, ma'am?" He spoke politely and tried to meet her eyes. Elizabeth could see at a glance that the left eye was focused on her while the other was off to the right.

Still a little frightened, Elizabeth stepped out of the stream, but continued to hold the mud-dripping pan to her chest. "I'm Elizabeth McRae. You might know my husband, Thornton McRae." She hoped the use of her husband's name might help to insure her safety. The stranger's hair was shoulder length, blond, and stringy. His clothing looked as if it could use a good scrubbing.

"I know ole Trap, ma'am. I shorely know him. But you can't be his wife. Can you?" he added doubtfully, with a slow and halting manner of speech.

"We've not been married long. What did you say your name is?"

"Muh name's Deck, ma'am. Some people call me Half-Deck, but I'm not sure why. You can just call me Deck. I hope I didn't skeer you too bad—" He stopped, looking apologetic.

Suddenly, Elizabeth was not afraid anymore. "Deck, you just startled me. I thought I was alone out here." She smiled at him, and he smiled back shyly.

"If you want some hep with that pannin' you're doin', I'm the one to ast. See up there in the shadders under them trees?" He pointed upstream. "That's where you ought to be workin'. That there big rock just below them shallows will make sure that anythang in the water is gonna settle in that little sink hole, at least fer a little while."

"Thanks, I'll try it up there." Then she remembered her manners. "You must be hungry. It's close to noon."

"I am that, ma'am."

"I'll see what I can find to eat. Come along."

Deck reached behind a tree where he had propped an aging rifle. He whistled and a mule appeared from the shadows of the forest. "Let's go, Pete," he said to the mule.

It turned out Deck's advice was correct. Within the next few days, Deck managed to turn up a few particles, and the sight of the first golden flecks was a thrill to Elizabeth as she watched Deck expertly sloshing the pan to and fro. They kept busy, with Deck showing her the best places up and down the stream and teaching her the correct way to swirl the pan with the least effort in order to separate the silt and sediment.

Deck made his home among the hills and the trees, rarely staying in one spot very long. She told him he was welcome to bunk in the horse shed. Elizabeth never knew for sure that he would be there from one day to the next, but he kept returning. Some days, Elizabeth would find that Deck had disappeared early in the morning, but he always returned late in the evening, sometimes with game, sometimes without.

Deck didn't fully understand what kept him coming back day after day. But he had seldom been needed or appreciated, mostly tolerated, at the mining camps where he chose to spend a few days now and then in the presence of humanity. Elizabeth's warmth and her appreciation of his help had him captivated.

Elizabeth was indeed grateful for his knowledge of the streams and the meat he provided, but she also enjoyed his company. He was never talkative, and their communication was similar to that between Elizabeth and Millie. Elizabeth would speak, Millie would respond with a snort or a friendly glance or perhaps not respond at all. Deck would usually respond with a nod of his head, maybe a smile, and maybe not at all—it was an easy relationship with no demands expressed or implied.

Elizabeth was frequently tempted to ride into Elk Fork, particularly on Sunday. She wanted to attend church, but any trip into town would mean questions about her husband and more lies for her to tell in order to keep up pretenses. Instead, she turned the pages of her Bible, reading favorite passages and humming her most-loved hymns while sitting on the front step in the sunlight. Even though Trap was gone, she was almost as restricted to home as she had been before.

One such Sunday, when she had put her Bible away and was coming back from the stream, carrying a bucket of water, she heard the hoofbeats of a lone horse coming slowly up the lane. She dashed inside with the water bucket and peered into the mirror, fluffing her hair where it had become tight little tendrils clinging to the perspiration on her forehead.

The horse and rider were coming into the front yard by the time she appeared on the front porch. The man looked familiar to her as he dismounted, then she recognized him and stepped onto the grass with a greeting.

"You're Brother Glover!"

"That I am, Sister McRae," he said as he tied his horse to a nearby tree.

"Please come in!" She stepped back and motioned toward the door. "I'm pleased to see you, although Mr. McRae is not at home." Then she could have bitten her tongue, realizing she had just told a lie on the Lord's Day. Actually, if there had been any way she could have hidden from the preacher, she would have done so, had she heard him coming in time.

"It's a warm day, ma'am. Why don't we just sit here on the porch. There's a good breeze out here."

The sun had moved behind a large pine, and the porch was in shade.

She thought rapidly of what she could offer him for refreshments, and her mind came up almost a blank. "I could put on a pot of coffee if you would care for some."

"No, ma'am, thank you. But a drink of water would be welcome." He tried to put her at ease as he sat down on the edge of the porch. "You've got an awful pretty place here. Nice trees."

When Herman Glover heard that Trap McRae had gone "prospecting," he guessed the truth. He had put off approaching Elizabeth McRae, hoping she would come into town for church services where he could speak to her afterward. Now he wasn't sure that he should have come to see her. The questions he had so carefully formulated in his mind to draw the truth from her seemed awkward and careless. He brushed off an imaginary piece of lint from his preaching slacks and cleared his throat.

"Sister McRae, I've been hopin' to see you in our congregation on Sundays. I hope you wasn't waitin' for an invitation, but I know I should've been out here before."

Elizabeth replied politely, "Well, I thank you for thinking of me. I intend to start coming to church, but I haven't quite got used to my horse just yet and thought it best if I stay close to home with her for a while." Lest he think her an unreligious woman, she added, "I read my Bible regularly, and I do miss services, Brother Glover."

Her last comment held such a sincere tone, he immediately responded in the same way. "I would be happy to come out on Sunday morning and escort you into town. It is a long ride for a lady alone."

"How kind of you to offer, but that won't be necessary. Millie and I will be used to each other soon, and you can count on seeing me regularly."

"After the trip you made to get to Elk Fork, I don't guess five miles or so means much. Why don't you tell me something about your life before you came here? We've all heard a little about you women, but I'd like to hear more about how you came to be here." Brother Glover was thinking it might make the basis for a good sermon recognizing the courage of the women of Elk Fork.

Elizabeth proceeded briefly to tell him her life's story, feeling that as a minister he had a right to ask.

Thinking that he had her on the correct, reflective path, Glover decided that it was best to be direct. "Has McRae left you, ma'am? I ask only because I want to be of any help to you that I can, as a servant of the Lord."

Elizabeth knew she could not lie to this man. Reluctantly, she answered. "Brother Glover, what we discuss, can this be strictly between the two of us?"

"A preacher never tells what has been told to him in private."

"Brother Glover, I think he has left me for good, but I can make it on my own." She tried to explain the relationship, or lack of one, as clearly as she could.

Herman Glover sat quietly until she finished with the statement, "I did the best I knew to do, but it wasn't enough, I guess." It was difficult for Herman Glover to respond in the manner of a minister. He wanted to put his arms around her and stroke her hair, but he restrained himself.

"Miz McRae, I will not say any harmful words about Trap, but you must not blame yourself. He's led an honest life, and he's tried to make it as a miner. But it seems it just ain't in 'im."

"What will I do, Brother Glover, if he comes back and wants this cabin? I suppose I can go somewhere else, but should I just leave this place to him? I've come to love it here."

"I don't think you need to worry about losing your home." Herman Glover wanted to tell her that he was pretty certain that if she stayed on at the place she would never have to worry about Trap McRae showing up again. Instead he said, "I hate to sound nosy, but do you have money to live on for a while?"

"Yes, I will be all right. Thank you for asking."

When Herman Glover had taken his leave, she continued to sit on the porch until she saw Deck approaching on Pete, holding up a wild turkey he had shot.

CHAPTER 11

"DECK," ELIZABETH ANNOUNCED one night a supper, "It's time for some new clothes for you. Let's go to town tomorrow." She hoped this would encourage Deck to stay on for a while. "You need a new blanket or two as well."

Deck responded with a smile and a nod of his head as he speared another biscuit with his fork.

That night she pulled out what was left of the fifty dollars that Betsy had returned to her after the purchase of the horse. There was not much left, since necessities purchased now and then at Barnes Emporium had depleted the funds. She sighed, knowing it was time to get into her other stash of money. Pulling the trunk out from under the bed, she thought it felt lighter than she remembered. Throwing the top open, she found that the coat in which she had placed the money was not there! Her boots were lying in one corner. There was a piece of coarse paper sticking out of the top of one. It was a single square of paper wrapped tightly around some object. Her fingers tore at it. Something was written on the inside of the paper. Smoothing it out, she slowly deciphered the crudely written message.

"Took your coat. Left money for another one."

The note was not signed, but she knew it was from Thornton McRae. She fingered a twenty-dollar gold piece, much more than the price of the coat itself, but the loss of the embroidered bag tucked inside the coat pocket brought tears to her eyes. Why would Thornton McRae have taken a woman's coat? Of course, it was wool and warm, something that could be used for a wrap against the weather, but hardly suitable for a hardened man of the mountains.

Elizabeth sat numbly, wondering how she was going to live now with nothing between her and starvation except a twenty-dollar gold piece, the few dollars she had left from the purchase of the horse, and maybe an ounce of gold dust. She became angry when she started to wonder what Trap thought she would live on when he abandoned her, and a hatred stirred her such as she had never felt before.

Finally she placed the gold piece in her valise and shoved the trunk back underneath the bed. Then she crept between the sheets.

It was a long night for Elizabeth. The wind raged through the trees and around the cabin, creating eerie noises as it forced its way through the cracks around the windows and the door. Sometime during the middle of the night, she arose and ran out to the horse shed where Deck slept. It seemed her hair might be torn from its roots and the clothing ripped from her body as she struggled against the wind that threatened to flatten the little shack where Deck and the horses slept. The moon and stars were bright in spite of the galelike strength against which she fought. It took little persuasion on her part to convince Deck to bring his blankets in to the hearth.

By morning, Elizabeth knew she could not force herself to make a trip into town. Deck did not seem particularly disappointed when she told him, feigning a headache as an excuse. But when the delay stretched into several days, Deck became concerned and limited his activities away from her to the procurement of food for the table.

Elizabeth was no longer full of high spirits when they went to the stream to seek a few flecks of gold. She went, she worked, but Deck could not see the spark of enjoyment she had shown in previous days. The creek had begun to dry up, so that there were only a few pools of water left that were deep enough for panning. Elizabeth tried to harvest from these pools daily in a frantic effort to obtain what little gold dust she could.

It was finally the sight of Deck in an old, frayed jacket against an early-morning chill that convinced her that she had to venture into town. Once again, she told Deck that they would be going into Elk Fork the following day.

During the night, wind blew in dark clouds, and the morning was cloudy and gray. A slight drizzle fell as Elizabeth and Deck mounted Millie and Pete and set out. Elizabeth dreaded the trip, especially since it had to be made in such weather, but she knew sleep would be easier when the business at hand was done.

They had traveled hardly a half mile on the road when they saw a rider coming toward them at a full gallop. He drew up as he approached them.

"Mrs. McRae, I was just headed for your place. Sheriff Barnes sent me. I was to tell you there's sign of Indians about! Sheriff Barnes said for you to stay close to that cabin of yours, or better still to come into town and stay with him and Miss Betsy or over at Ben's hotel rooms." Then he seemed to see Deck for the first time. "Deck, what are you doin' here?"

"I'm just ridin' with Miss Elizabeth," Deck responded in his usual matter-of-fact manner.

"Deck's been helping out at my place while Mr. McRae has been away, and a lot of help he has been too."

Deck stared modestly at Pete's ears, a smile playing at his mouth.

Elizabeth continued, "We were just riding into town for supplies and ammunition, especially ammunition now that you've given us this news. Think we'll be safe along this road?"

"You oughta be, ma'am. I'll ride back into town with you and come back out with you, too, if you need me. Deck here, though, knows Indian ways about as well as anybody around, except maybe your husband." The rider stopped abruptly and changed the subject.

"I'm Gene Chadron, ma'am. I saw you at the wedding ceremony." He removed his hat with a polite smile.

On the way into town, Elizabeth asked what he meant by "sign of Indians." She learned that Indians had been sighted twice; once by a lone hunter, who had been fired upon by a group of five or six braves as he stalked a deer. The other encounter occurred when a group of six men from Elk Fork had ridden out to scout around after the hunter had returned to town with his story.

"There was shooting, and we think our men must've hit one. There was a little blood on the ground." Gene Chadron sounded pleased.

Elizabeth felt grim when she entered Barnes Emporium, but she managed to put on a sprightly act and get right down to business.

"Mr. Barnes, when my husband left, he suggested I might be able to open a charge account with you. Of course, we will stand good for it when he returns."

"Ma'am, the pleasure is mine. You still want that kitten? It's about time to take him away from his mama."

"I do, indeed, Mr. Barnes."

She bought flour, coffee, sugar, baking powder, a blanket plus a jacket and a couple of changes of clothing for Deck, and a denim jacket for herself.

After Elizabeth made her purchases, Ben Barnes talked to her in a straightforward manner, trying not to arouse undue fear in her.

"Mrs. McRae, you will do right well to keep Deck around your place if you decide to stay there with this Indian trouble. It could be nothing, but if things get worse, if I was you, I'd come into town till things blow over. You know you're always welcome to use one of the rooms upstairs. Do you have a gun?"

"Mr. Barnes, I wouldn't know how to shoot a gun if I had one."

"Deck can teach you how."

"I can't afford a gun," she protested.

"Seems to me in this situation, you can't afford not to have one." He led her to the weapons display.

Elizabeth let herself be talked into buying a weapon and rode out of town with an old Sharps rifle across her knees. Deck accompanied her, proudly carrying his packet of new clothes tied together with twine.

CHAPTER 12

AS THE ROAD took a turn into thick pines, which shut Elk Fork off from view, Elizabeth had to admit to herself that she was frightened. The clouds still hung in close to the earth and mist drifted through the tops of the trees, though no rain fell. She shivered and pulled her new jacket more closely around her, upset that today's necessities and the used weapon had put her close to thirty dollars in debt. They wasted no time, but pushed along as fast as Deck could get Pete to move.

They had just come around a bend in the road when Deck spoke softly, "Miss Elizabeth, somethin' moved in them bushes up the way. Just act natural, like we ain't seen nothin' yet. I can't outrun anything on this durn mule. If it's Injuns, maybe I can talk us out of some trouble. If I can't, and I yell to you to run, you kick that horse with all yore might and head back down the trail to town. Now let's just go along slow 'n easy." He handed his packet of new clothes to Elizabeth. His old rifle lay across the neck of the mule, pointing almost unnoticeably toward the bushes to the left of the trail ahead.

As they rode along slowly, Elizabeth could pick out a dark brown patch that didn't fit in with the green of the scrub oak where it lay. She pointed with her hand and said to Deck, "My coat! That's my coat!"

"Well, somebody's wearin' it, Miss Elizabeth. It just moved," Deck whispered.

Deck stopped his mule short of whatever was in the scrub oak. He closely scanned the surrounding forest on both sides of the road. His experience with the mountain tribes told him this could be a trap, although he couldn't figure out why any Indian would want to bother with them. Motioning for Elizabeth to stay put, Deck swung one leg over the mule's head and slipped to the ground. Rifle ready, he crouched low and crept forward. When he got even with the form on the ground, he straightened, pointed his rifle, and with the toe of his boot gave a shove. The body flopped over, and he was looking down into the face of a young Indian woman whose eyelids fluttered a little.

"Miss Elizabeth, it's a woman! An Indian woman!" His voice held a tone of disbelief. "And she's been hurt!" He could see a big, brownish stain on her coat.

Elizabeth leaped from the horse and ran forward.

"We got to get 'er to town, Miss Elizabeth!"

Elizabeth knelt and felt the young woman's throat for a pulse. It was steady, but weak. The woman's eyelids were fluttering rapidly as if she struggled to regain consciousness; they would open briefly, then drift shut again.

"No, our place is closer; we're almost there. Let's get her to bed and then you can go for help." Elizabeth turned her attention to the Indian woman, speaking soothingly as she rubbed the woman's forehead, hoping to ease the fear that showed in her eyes each time she opened them.

Perhaps in response to the words and the stroking, perhaps not, the Indian woman finally opened her eyes and focused on Elizabeth's face. Elizabeth pushed her back as the woman began to struggle to rise.

"No, do not be afraid. We will help you." Elizabeth spoke slowly, hoping she would be understood. "We will take you to our house."

"No doctor." The woman's voice was almost a whisper, but her English was clear.

"No, there is no doctor there, but we will get one soon."

Elizabeth turned to Deck. "Do you think we could get her on Millie and you could take her to the house?"

"No need for Millie, ma'am. Ole Pete's shorter, and it'd be a sight easier to get her up on him." Deck spoke with the common sense that was characteristic of him. He proved right. Between the two of them, they got the Indian woman into Deck's arms astride the mule.

By the time they arrived at the cabin, the woman was more alert. As Deck carried her into the house, she motioned to be placed in front of the fireplace where a few coals were banked. Elizabeth spread a blanket down, and Deck eased her onto it as Elizabeth tucked a pillow underneath her head.

The woman smiled weakly in gratitude, then repeated her previous words, "No doctor."

"We can get a doctor for you from town." Actually, there was no doctor in town, but there was Mrs. Tupelo, the wife of an aging miner, a woman who had pried bullets out of men and babies out of women, and had treated various ailments much of her life.

The Indian woman winced as she forced herself up to lean on her elbows. "You do not understand. No one must know I am here. I cannot explain now. Let me rest. I will talk more later. Please." Her eyes as well as her voice were pleading.

"We will do as you wish for now. But you must let me examine your wound."

The woman nodded and tried to help Elizabeth remove the coat. Elizabeth wanted to jerk the coat off and check the pocket for her possessions, but she restrained herself. A sizable reddish-brown stain had soaked into the woolen fibers and made them stiff and crackly in Elizabeth's fingers. Underneath the coat, the woman was dressed in simple everyday attire of the whites: a coarse white blouse and a black print skirt with tiny red flowers. Like the coat, the blouse and upper portions of the skirt were caked with blood, some of it still bright and red just above the waistline. Elizabeth pulled up the bottom of the blouse to reveal an angry looking, festering wound just below the rib cage.

"I'll boil water to cleanse your wound and make something for you to eat," Elizabeth told her as she pulled the blouse down and tucked the sides of the blanket around the woman.

The Indian woman nodded and closed her eyes. Elizabeth quickly prepared a simple meal for herself and Deck and made a thick gravy for their visitor, who seemed to sleep as Elizabeth worked.

The woman was able to feed herself after she awoke and Elizabeth had bathed her wound. She motioned to Elizabeth to place the bowl of gravy on the floor beside her. Pushing herself up to lean on one elbow, she was able to spoon gravy and bits of bread into her mouth. She looked up questioningly between bites.

"Name?" she asked briefly.

"I'm Elizabeth McRae and this is Deck." She motioned toward Deck, who looked toward the woman with his good eye and a small, crooked smile.

When the gravy bowl was empty, the Indian woman leaned back against the pillow. "I know you have many questions which I cannot answer tonight."

There were many questions boiling in Elizabeth's mind, but she kept them to herself.

"I am Blue Flower of the Ute. Do you know of me?" She waited until Elizabeth shook her head. "I have traveled far. My wound is nothing. Made me bleed much. Tomorrow I will be better. We can talk then. May I ask that tonight you let no one know of me?"

"Of course. If you are sure you do not need a doctor," Elizabeth replied, fighting curiosity.

"Your man"—she nodded toward Deck, who sat self-consciously finishing his coffee—"he must go back where you found me and wipe out anything to show I was there—

blood, crushed grasses, horse prints. Tomorrow, I can explain."

"Deck is not—Deck is a friend who is working for me," Elizabeth wanted to clear up any idea that Deck was her "man." "He is wise in the ways of the woods. He will go out as you asked, if he thinks it is safe, and erase the tracks and signs of your presence." She look questioningly at Deck.

"Yes, ma'am. From what she says it seems the safest thing to do. Somebody's follerin' her, and we don't know who. I'll keep a close eye on things tonight. I'm already feelin' a little spooked. Couldn't sleep anyway."

"Can I keep watch for you part of the night?" Elizabeth was beginning to feel tingles of fear.

"No, ma'am, Ole Pete's the only backup I need. He's helped me keep watch for Injuns, grizzlies, wolves. He's better'n most men. 'Fore I go out, let me show you a thing or two about that Sharps you bought. I'll show you how it works, and you don't need to worry much about aimin'. If you hear or see somethin', just make sure it ain't me, point the gun in that direction, and go to firin'."

His words didn't do much to calm Elizabeth's nerves, but they made her glad she had succumbed to Ben Barnes's persuasion and had bought the rifle.

It was not quite nightfall when Deck slipped outside to comply with Blue Flower's request.

As soon as he was out the door, Elizabeth propped the Sharps close by and carried the lamp from the kitchen table into the bedroom. She had thrown the coat casually across the bed when she had taken it off the Indian woman. Now she clutched at it and stuck her hand into the deep pocket. She felt the embroidered bag and pulled out the familiar contents: her mother's faded letter, the leather pouch that held her mother's treasured carving of the bear, the small hand-painted portrait of her youthful parents, and the money. She counted it, and it was all there, down to the last dollar.

Elizabeth went in to stir the fire once more. The evenings were getting cold and told her that there would probably be a short fall before winter descended upon them.

Questions plagued her mind as she sat for some time, staring at the young Indian woman. How was it that this Blue Flower was wearing her coat? How and why had she turned up here? She studied the woman's face. Blue Flower was not beautiful, but she was attractive, with rather prominent features. For some reason she could not define, Elizabeth saw a strength of character. Soon, though, her ability to wonder and question played itself out, and feeling exhausted, she retired to her bed.

It must have been three, maybe four, hours later that Elizabeth was awakened by loud groans and incoherent noises from the other room. Grabbing her nightrobe, Elizabeth rushed in to find Blue Flower thrashing about on the blanket, speaking in a language Elizabeth could not understand. A hand pressed to Blue Flower's forehead told Elizabeth she was burning with fever. She ran to the door. Opening it, she stepped outside and yelled, "Deck, it's me. I'm coming out."

"Yes, ma'am. I'm over here."

She dashed for the shed through the mist that still drifted close to the ground. It was impossible to see Deck in the darkness of the shed, but she followed his voice as he called softly to her.

"Deck, the Indian woman is delirious with fever. In spite of her wishes, I think we've got to get Mrs. Tupelo up here. Could you take Millie and go for her?" Before he could answer, she continued. "Let me tell you about this coat she was wearing." Elizabeth told him the whole story, but carefully omitted the amount of cash that had been in the pocket.

Deck was often slow to respond, and he took a little bit longer than usual now. "I'd been wonderin' what you meant about the coat bein' yores. Figgered it had been stole. I don't know what to make of this story. But I guess for now the best to be done is to git Miz Tupelo. Chances are I could break her fever, but Miz Tupelo's prob'ly the best bet. I hate to leave you alone in the middle of the night, but it's safest fer you now. Injuns don't like to attack at night if they's no good reason fer it. You just take old Pete, put a rope on 'im, and tie 'im by the door. You set inside with that gun. Pete'll let you know if anybody comes prowlin' aroun'." In the darkness, he groped for Pete's rope and shoved it toward her. "You just spray the woods good with that gun if anybody comes aroun'. When me 'n Miz Tupelo ride in, I'll give old Pete the signal that it's me."

"Indians? Deck, do you think Indians might be out there?"

"No, ma'am, I don't think there's Injuns out there. But it pays to be careful. We got one Indian here, an' where they's one, they's likely to be a passel of 'em."

"Why would they attack here? We're trying to help this woman!"

"Some men can't be predicted, and somebody shot 'er. We don't know who."

She put the rope on Pete and led him to a small pine outside the front door where she tied him while Deck hurriedly saddled Millie. He was off without a good-bye, riding silently into the mist.

She recognized Millie's pace when she heard the horse trotting up the lane. It was shortly after daybreak when the sound awoke her from a light sleep in the chair pulled next to the door. Opening the door a crack and peering out, Elizabeth could see that Pete was complacent where he stood. As Millie and Deck came into view, she rushed out the door.

"Deck, where is Mrs. Tupelo? Is she coming?"

Deck shook his head as he got off the horse and led her to the shed.

Elizabeth held her questions, knowing Deck would get his answer together as soon as he could. He led the horse to the shed and began wiping her down with a frayed, gray rag.

"Miss Elizabeth, Miz Tupelo wouldn't come. Said she wasn't gonna risk comin' out here for a danged Indian woman when the Injuns are ridin' through this country like they owned it, shootin' at whites an' all." He continued to rub down the horse, and it seemed he couldn't stop talking.

"She said too that she wasn't makin' no calls out here, because you're a friend of that woman that's singin' now in the saloon." He stopped to wipe his nose. "Since you tole me the story about that there coat, I figgered out who this woman is. Ma'am, I mean no disrespect, but that there is Trap McRae's Indian woman. He must've took the coat to 'er. I ain't figgered out yet how she got here with it," he finished weakly.

Elizabeth tried to sort out what she had just heard, but shortly put aside thoughts of Thornton McRae to deal with the more urgent situation. "Well, whatever is going on, we must help Blue Flower. You said something last night about being able to break her fever?"

"I kin try. I seen some Indian horsemint not too far away if I kin just recollect where it is. It usually cuts a fever if you brew it up in hot water."

"Let me get breakfast for you and then you can try to find the horsemint. Deck"—she tried to question gently for she could see that his nerves were as raw-edged as hers—"did you have a chance to talk to Sheriff Red Barnes about this?"

"Well, no, ma'am, I guess I didn't. I tried to, but Miss Betsy tole me he was out lookin' fer Injuns. Guess I should'a tried to find somebody else. I was so danged worried, I just rid out'a town and didn't do it."

"It's all right, Deck. Probably wouldn't have helped much anyway. We'll get Blue Flower out of the fever. Deck . . . what did you mean that this is Mr. McRae's Indian woman?"

"I shouldn't 'a mentioned that. I guess it just spurted out."

"Well, since it started spurting, why don't you tell me what you were talking about?" Elizabeth tried to make it as easy as possible for him. "I've read that white men sometimes take Indian women as wives when they live in the mountains. Is this what you mean about Blue Flower?" It was hard for her to put into words, but she knew it would be more difficult for Deck to do so.

"Yes, ma'am, I guess that's what I mean." Deck seemed ready to burst into tears as he hid his face against Millie's neck.

"Deck, I understand. There was not much between Mr. McRae and myself anyway." She tried to make him feel better. "You finish with the horse while I get breakfast for you. You did a good job tonight, and a dangerous one. I appreciate what you did."

He nodded his head up and down against Millie's neck.

CHAPTER 13

BREAKFAST WAS HARDLY over when they heard several horses riding hard toward the cabin. Deck grabbed his rifle. Elizabeth, though pale, put a hand out to stop him. "Wait, let's see who it is."

Together they opened a shutter and peered out. Six white men pulled up their horses as they rode into the clearing.

"Let me try to handle this. They won't shoot a woman." Elizabeth, of course, could not recognize a face among them as she stepped out onto the porch, her rifle underneath her arm as much for show as anything.

"Good morning, gentlemen," she shouted across the clearing. "What brings you this way?" The confident ring of her voice surprised her, since she was shaking inside.

The men looked like miners, dressed in blue denim and rough jackets. Some had knit caps pulled over their ears against the chill of the morning.

One man rode his horse forward a few paces. "We're here for the Indian woman."

Elizabeth did not even have to think about her reply. "Then be on your way. She is ill and will stay here until she is better."

The forward rider paced his horse toward the house. "We're here for the woman," he repeated. "There's an Indian war going on around here, you fool!"

Elizabeth's temper flared. She had never been addressed in such a denigrating way before. Pointing the gun toward him, she motioned for Deck to join her on the porch. "You've no right on this property. I've a sick woman here and this is where she stays!" Surprising herself, she aimed the Sharps toward the sky and fired for emphasis. She heard Deck cock his gun beside her.

The forward rider sat a moment, staring at Elizabeth and Deck. "We could rush you, you know, but we don't want to hurt a white woman. We'll give you time to think it over. We'll be back for the Indian woman soon."

Elizabeth's hands were shaking so she could hardly hold the rifle. As the men turned and rode away, she walked inside to see Blue Flower rolling back and forth restlessly on the blanket before the fire. Kneeling close to her on the floor, Elizabeth stroked the woman's brow. "Deck, I don't know what to do first. We need something to break her fever, but we also need to notify Sheriff Barnes about this threat. I don't understand why they want this woman. And how did they know she's here?"

"Miz Tupelo has always talked too much. You can count on her gaddin' about, spreadin' the word as soon as I left town. Them drunks could've got wind of it without no trouble. Anythang that happens gets heard about in the Wet Whistle first off."

He was quiet for a moment or two, frowning as if in thought, one eye looking at the Indian woman and the other staring across the room. "I seem to recollect that maybe that Indian horsemint was over by that big holler tree just north of here. That would break her fever fast, a little horsemint tea. I could go see if I kin find it if you'll be all right here fer a little bit. I doubt them men will come back fer a while."

"That sounds like the best idea, Deck. Let me ask you something before you go. Do you know if those men are from around here? Did you recognize any of them?"

"Nary a one. They wasn't Elk Fork regulars. Probably, they come down from the hills to get in a little Injun hunt-in' and a little drinkin'."

"Why would they want the Indian woman? Obviously, she hasn't been out shooting at white men."

Deck's face started to turn red, and he hesitated before speaking. "They's some white men, Miss Elizabeth, that would, well, they'd use any reason they could come up with to, uh, well, to get to an Indian woman."

Elizabeth stared at him a moment before she began to understand the meaning of his stammering words. It was her turn to feel her face turning crimson. She could not respond to such a horrible concept.

"You go on and see if you can find the horsemint. You're probably right—those men won't be back for a while. I'll keep a close watch." Elizabeth wanted to cry, but she kept a straight face until Deck was out of sight. Then a few tears coursed down her face and dripped off her chin.

Deck was back in less than an hour, and Blue Flower had already seemed to calm down a little. Her pulse was not racing as fast, and she was resting more quietly. Elizabeth had been moving from the window to the water bucket, to the woman's side, placing fresh, wet rags on her face and chest with every trip back and forth.

Elizabeth had a kettle of water boiling on the fire; when Deck arrived, he tossed a large handful of leaves, stems, and roots into the pot. Almost at once, a fragrance of the forest filled the room. Within a half hour, Elizabeth was spooning tea into Blue Flower as she swallowed, moaned, and protested that she wanted to sleep.

"At least she knows that she should speak in English," Elizabeth commented to Deck. "I think she's beginning to get the better of this fever."

After Blue Flower had finished taking the tea and had fallen asleep, Elizabeth spoke to Deck. "I guess it might be too soon for you to be able to find Red Barnes back in town. Rest awhile, and we'll see what this tea does for Blue Flower."

While Deck and Blue Flower slept, Elizabeth and Pete kept watch.

It must have been close to midnight when Deck rapped softly on the door. Elizabeth heard his footsteps on the porch and sat up, instantly alert.

"Miss Elizabeth, it's me. Let me in."

When she opened the door, Deck look flustered. "Them men are camped down close to the road!"

"The men? You mean the ones that came for Blue Flower this morning?"

"Them's the ones. I woke up and couldn't get back to sleep so I thought I'd slip aroun' awhile and see what I could find in the woods. I do that sometimes you know," he added defensively.

"Of course, Deck. Go on, tell me about this encampment."

"Well, it's the same ones as we saw this mornin'. And they're drinkin' hard. Kind of skeered me to watch 'em."

"Then they might come up here anytime, and there are too many of them for us." Elizabeth's mind was racing. She knew she could not let Deck try to get to Sheriff Barnes now and leave her and the Indian woman alone to face six men who might come upon the cabin anytime.

Deck's mind was working too. "It's not safe here, Miss Elizabeth, for the Indian woman, and maybe not even you. Comin' back through the woods, I had an idea. I know a cave not too far from here. I don't think many white men know about it, and maybe not many Indians even. If we could get Blue Flower on the horse, I could take you there if you want me to. You'd be safe. We could prob'ly be there by mornin'."

Elizabeth walked over to the fire and stood, studying the flames. "Can't we get to town? There must be some back way where we can keep away from those men."

"No, ma'am, I don't think that's a good idea. We best

clear out to the north." Deck kept his eyes cast on the floor. He hated to keep the truth from Elizabeth, but he could see the strain she was under and thought it best not to tell the whole story. While Elizabeth had thought he slept, Deck had made forays in each direction after grabbing an hour or so of rest. Slipping through a midnight forest was perhaps Deck's greatest skill. It had certainly proved to be a valuable asset tonight when he had found a remuda of a dozen or so Indian ponies to the east, perhaps two miles from Elizabeth's cabin. He had not gone in close enough to count the Indians sleeping around the fire. Circling back while planning a retreat to Elk Fork for the three of them, he had come upon the white men. He knew he dared not lead the women to town through the woods because of the thick underbrush on the downward slope of the mountain. To the north they would travel through the large pines that forested the upper slope, making travel swift and quiet.

Elizabeth had learned to trust Deck when it came to conditions in the mountains. "Do you think Blue Flower can travel?" The Indian woman had been quietly sleeping for several hours now.

"If she can't ride, I can tie her on the horse."

"All right, then let's pack a few things." Elizabeth started gathering food while Deck tied his packs onto Pete. She insisted upon bringing her valise with personal articles and an extra change of clothing. Patiently, Deck added them to Pete's burden.

In less than a half hour, they were on their way. Elizabeth and Blue Flower were astride Millie, the half-conscious Indian woman in front, leaning against Elizabeth. A three-quarter moon lighted the way through the tall pines as though it were near daylight instead of the middle of the night. Deck led the way astride Pete, picking his way carefully where the least sign of their passing would remain, yet traveling with steady speed.

Instead of tying the Indian woman to the saddle, Deck and Elizabeth had placed a rope around the waists of the two women, binding them together for Blue Flower's safety. Elizabeth held onto Millie's reins with her right hand and clutched Blue Flower against her with her left. Her hips hung painfully over the back of the cantle. Although the horse was traveling at only a swift pace, Elizabeth felt the Indian woman sway to and fro, dangerously close to pulling both of them from the saddle. With feet braced firmly in the stirrups, Elizabeth tried to hold herself erect with the weight pulling at her as Blue Flower bobbed and weaved.

Occasionally, a knifelike gust of wind would strike Elizabeth, almost tossing her from the saddle. Elizabeth's courage weakened when she thought about riding through the darkness, fighting the tearing, ripping wind, but the gusts soon lessened, then stopped altogether. The night became still, almost frighteningly still. It seemed to Elizabeth that each footstep the animals made must be echoing all the way down to Elk Fork.

Elizabeth's eyes moved constantly through the trees, and she caught her breath more than once when a shadow seemed to take the form of a human or she caught some movement from the changing patterns of light as they passed a few aspen with their leaves glimmering in the moonlight and quaking in spite of the stillness around them. The night air grew cooler, and Elizabeth shivered inside the blanket she had wrapped around her. Blue Flower was again wearing Elizabeth's coat and made a shield of warmth in front of her. To Elizabeth, it seemed they were wandering aimlessly through the trees, but she was confident that Deck had his sense of direction correct.

As the moon began to slant down sharply, they came upon a trail. Deck turned Pete to the left, and Elizabeth could see a steep climb ahead of them along a path that must once have been well-worn, but which now was covered with deep, foot-high grass.

"Deck," Elizabeth whispered, just loud enough to be heard.

Deck was riding maybe five feet ahead. He halted Pete. "Yes, ma'am, is somethin' wrong?"

"Is this an Indian trail?"

"A old one. You can see it ain't been used much lately."

"But since there's Indian trouble around, what if they decide to use it now. What if we run upon them?"

"Well, ain't much use runnin', unless they're afoot." He didn't add that there was no safe place to run to anyway. "If we see any Injuns, they'd like be Ute. Maybe they'd take kindly to us since we're helpin' Blue Flower." He turned straight ahead again and urged Pete on, hoping he had helped to lessen Elizabeth's worries about the trail. It was the least of his worries.

The little party came close to the peak of a ridge, but Deck stopped before they reached it. Stopping just off the trail, underneath several large pines, he jumped off Pete. When the steady movement of the horse ceased, Blue Flower began to stir, as a baby does when its cradle stills. Her head jerked up, and she looked around.

"Where is this place?" Blue Flower's body tensed, and she sounded disoriented.

Elizabeth hoped she would not begin to fight when she realized the two of them were bound together.

"Blue Flower, it's all right. Keep still."

"We're out in the middle of the woods, Blue Flower. You probably know the place by name. We're close to Wolf Point," Deck explained.

Blue Flower nodded slightly, and Elizabeth could feel her body relax.

"Miss Elizabeth, I know you must be awful saddle worn, but I'm afraid to get her off where you can walk around some. I ain't sure how much luck we'd have gettin' her back up on the horse."

"I can get up." Blue Flower surprised them with her response. "I am tired. Weak. But I can get back on the horse."

Deck untied the rope binding them together and pulled Blue Flower to the ground. She lay there, flexing her legs gently while Elizabeth dismounted stiffly.

"That there's Wolf Point, ma'am." Deck pointed to a craggy outcropping of granite that Elizabeth could make out only because it was white against a now dark and moonless sky.

"I'm gonna go up and take a look. I can see just about anything around from up there, and hear it too. Sounds carry up to that point like the wind was bringin' 'em to ye."

Elizabeth walked silently about while Deck crept up to the massive rock and flattened himself on its outer edges.

When Deck returned, he offered both women a drink of water from the canteen he took from Pete's packs. Then he explained, "Couldn't see or hear nothin'. But just to be safe, we're takin' to the trees agin. It's easy travelin' up on that ridge, but we don't want to take the chance of bein' seen."

"Being seen in this darkness?" Elizabeth had been mostly feeling her way around the horse as she paced.

"I know it's darker'n the inside of a buffalo's belly, but we ain't takin' no chances. We're gonna be close to the top of the ridge, but just down in the trees a little."

"How much farther to go?" All this seemed unreal to Elizabeth, but her fears had lessened with every mile they put between themselves and the encampment near the cabin.

"I told you we'd be there by mornin' and it looks like I'll be close to right. Not much more than a couple of hours, I'd guess."

Two more hours in the saddle seemed as much as a lifetime to Elizabeth at this point with her legs still weak and trembling. But she mounted up, drawing Blue Flower close once again. As her fear diminished some, she pondered the presence of Blue Flower. Why she had turned up near Elk Fork? Who pursued the woman? Where was Thornton McRae? Elizabeth finally gave up those thoughts in order to concentrate on being able to discern Pete's dark rump as the trees grew thicker.

Elizabeth soon saw that it would be almost impossible for anyone to accidentally stumble upon the place they were headed. They wound through the trees as if Deck followed a mental map. Finally, the darkness began to turn to a gray dawn and Elizabeth could see they were traveling up a gully on the side of the mountain. The trees had given way to boulders and stones, evidence that this was a springtime wash that carried the runoff of melting snows. Millie picked her way carefully, placing each hoof slowly between rocks where footing was sure. Deck stopped and dropped off the mule's back.

"Miss Elizabeth, we've gotta go up here." He motioned toward a steep incline just to his right, covered with slippery shale.

"Deck! We can't get Millie up that slope! She'll break a leg!"

"She'll do fine. I'm gonna tie her to ole Pete, and she'll foller along like a puppy. Only problem is, you ladies can't ride up."

"I wouldn't ride a horse up that for anything! I'm not sure I could even crawl up that hillside!"

"Well, you ain't gonna have to. You see them rocks up ahead? Climbin' them is easy—for people, that is. Git down and set right here. I'll lead ole Pete and Millie up, then I'll be right back down to help you and Blue Flower up them rocks, even if I have to carry you one at a time." As he spoke, he was untying the rope that bound the women together.

Deck sounded so positive, Elizabeth's courage rose. "You won't need to carry me if you'll give me a few minutes to limber up my legs."

Blue Flower even rallied to the challenge, "I might have to crawl, but I can make it, too."

Deck was right about the horse. With Deck leading Pete and Pete pulling Millie, the three of them made it to the top of the slope without mishap, although Millie's eyes were rolling with nervousness and she strained against the persistent tugging from the stout mule. Deck scurried back down, smoothing the shale as best he could behind him to obliterate the deep gouges the animals had made.

In spite of her best efforts, Blue Flower was too weak to scale the boulders up the hillside. Between the two of them, Elizabeth and Deck pushed, pulled, and half-carried the woman to the top. The morning sun was beginning to touch the tops of the peaks, bringing a welcome warmth. The air was thin near the top of the mountain; Elizabeth sat down, leaning against a massive rock and breathing heavily.

"How much farther now?"

"We're here. This is as far as we go."

Elizabeth sat up and looked around. "I thought we were going to a cave for shelter."

"Yes, ma'am." Deck smiled impishly, his good eye focused on her face. "You're 'bout there. You could throw a rock an' hit it. Rest a minute, then I'll show ya."

Indeed, Deck soon showed them to their shelter, well hidden on the mountainside. Facing the cave to which Deck led them, no one would have guessed that there was a break in the sheer rock wall. Massive boulders partially concealed the entrance, which could only be seen by approaching from the south where the rock formed a natural entryway into the hillside chamber.

It took a few moments for Elizabeth's eyes to adjust to the semidarkness within. She stood, looking about, as Deck lay Blue Flower, still wrapped in the coat, on a blanket in the corner near the entrance.

"This place is huge!" Elizabeth had been anticipating a small cubbyhole where she and Blue Flower would hole up like gophers in a burrow. The interior of the cave was as large as a Bostonian living room, with the back tapering off into tunnellike darkness. She looked about apprehensively, seeking the bats or snakes that might be sharing the space within.

"Yes, ma'am. They's enough room for all of us." He was tugging at Pete's rope, coaxing the mule inside.

"You're bringing the animals inside?" Elizabeth turned with surprise to see Pete and Millie joining them.

Deck hesitated only momentarily. "Well, yes, Miss Elizabeth, I wanna keep 'em outta sight till I'm sure we wasn't follered. An' they gotta stay in here at night because we can't leave 'em outside fer the varmints to get at. They's a good stand of grass not more'n a few steps away. I'll go cut a couple of handfuls soon's I get a fire goin'."

Elizabeth was exhausted. She sat down near Blue Flower and pulled a blanket around her shoulders. Without realizing it, she leaned back against the rock wall of the cave, asleep almost before she touched it.

Elizabeth awoke sometime later to the sound of Millie and Pete grinding sweet grass noisily. Deck was hunkered over a small fire at the entrance to the cave. A small pile of stones held a pan filled with water, and Deck was tossing the leaves and stems of horsemint into it. He looked around when she stirred.

"Makin' us some tea. Her fever's broke good, but she needs some more tea to keep it down. An' a little of it won't hurt us neither. We better not cook and risk smoke till night. I oughtta be able to snare us a couple of rabbits by then."

Elizabeth's insides were groaning with hunger. She accepted the tea and a few strips of jerky gratefully, then fell asleep again. She slept long and hard and awoke early in the evening to the sizzle of rabbit frying. Joining Deck by the fire outside, she apologized, "I didn't mean to sleep so long. I guess you got those rabbits you were talking about."

"They was easy, almost beggin' to be caught."

She looked toward their sizzling supper. "You packed lard and a frying pan?"

"I always travel with lard and a fryin' pan. Sometimes the lard melts in hot weather and dribbles down Pete's sides, an' that kind of makes him mad. But then there's lots of thangs that makes Pete mad. I guess lard drippin' down his sides is one of the worst, though."

Deck always had a way of putting things into perspective for Elizabeth, and it was the same now as she sat looking out over the forest and wondering just how she had come to be in this place and this predicament. But it was still better than Boston.

"Seems like Blue Flower is sleeping."

"She has been ever' time I looked in on her. She'll be good as new in a day or so, I reckon."

"Deck, don't you ever sleep?"

"Yes, ma'am."

She waited for him to explain. He didn't. She asked. "When do you sleep? You seem always to be awake and looking out for things."

"Well, I slept a little under a tree whilst I was waitin' fer these rabbits."

He said no more, and Elizabeth gave up the conversation.

As night moved in, Elizabeth awoke Blue Flower. She seemed stronger, and the three of them chewed on the tough fried rabbit and some biscuits that Elizabeth had brought from the cabin. There was little conversation, no discussion of what their next plans were. They were dog-tired and welcomed the concealing safety of darkness. Elizabeth fell asleep determined to get some answers from Blue Flower in the morning.

Breakfast was cooked before good daylight could arrive to reveal what little smoke Deck's dry firewood produced. The meal was surprisingly good, leftover rabbit and a thick gravy that Deck had stirred up from last night's skillet drippings, accompanied by somewhat stale bread brought with them.

"Tonight we'll have fresh biscuits fer supper," Deck announced as he began to dig a hole in the hard soil just outside the cave.

"We have no milk. How can you make biscuits without milk?"Elizabeth queried.

"Water," Deck replied simply. "Just add more bakin' powder. They won't be as light and fluffy as yore mama likely made, but they'll be tolerable good."

Deck showed her how to place the coals from the fire inside the hole he had dug. When he had finished mixing the batter, he rolled little balls of dough into biscuits and placed them inside the heavy iron skillet, which he then covered with an equally heavy lid. He placed the skillet in the hole, then covered it with coals and, finally, a thick covering of soil. The biscuits were cooking before the morning sun rose above the peak to the east.

Deck felt confident that they had not been followed, since his morning search of the area had revealed nothing to indicate the presence of mankind. After he had picketed Millie and Pete outside and brought fresh water from the nearby spring, Elizabeth cautiously broached the subject that had been on her mind since she awoke.

"Blue Flower, do you feel like telling us your story?"

"Yes, I must," she agreed.

CHAPTER 14

BLUE FLOWER HAD been braiding her hair when she learned that Thornton McRae was approaching her village. Three teenaged boys who had been out for an early morning hunt rushed toward her as she sat outside her tepee, each trying to be first to tell her that her white man was back. She tried not to show surprise or alarm, but continued to braid slowly and calmly. Blue Flower knew the boys were excited, not because Thornton McRae was returning, but because there would soon be a confrontation between McRae and Night Wind.

As soon as the boys left, disappointed that they had got no reaction from Blue Flower, she picked up her baby of three months, Little Eagle—Night Wind's son—and called to Thorn Dove, who had been wrestling with a couple of the dogs. Gathering her children to her, she entered her lodge, thankful that Night Wind was away. She only wished that he were gone for more than a brief hunting expedition.

Blue Flower knew that as soon as the news spread through the village she could expect a visit from Night Wind's father, Sacred Moon, who was their leader. She added twigs to the fire and prepared to heat water for tea. She had not long to wait.

Her lodge was open, and she was sitting in front of the door when Sacred Moon approached. He walked slowly, bent over and aided by a rod of cedar. Previously a man of height, he had now only to dip his head a little to enter through the low doorway the folded-back flap provided. The old man's instructions were clear: Thornton McRae would be welcomed into the village, but Blue Flower and Thorn Dove were strictly forbidden to meet with him. McRae would be accepted as a respected guest from the past, but the hospitality would not be extended to encourage him to stay. Blue Flower understood and promised to keep the children inside. Sacred Moon left.

She complied with her promise and kept the flap to her tepee shut. Sitting in the delicate light that the fibrous walls admitted, she entertained Thorn Dove and Little Eagle, wanting the day to end but dreading the knowledge that Thornton McRae was out of her life forever. She also feared for his safety should Night Wind return and find him in their midst.

Night Wind was a good provider for the family, but he flogged Blue Flower regularly when he found her musing, and he accused her of thinking of Thornton McRae. His jealousy of the white man was acute. Before the birth of Little Eagle, when it had become apparent that Blue Flower was with child, Night Wind had become more gentle with her, yet he was always sharp with Thorn Dove, sometimes slapping the child for no apparent reason.

The birth of Little Eagle had done nothing to soften Night Wind's nature. It seemed his son brought a renewed desire to make war on the whites with extraordinary energy. His warlike nature had brought him into many conflicts with Sacred Moon, who was a peace-loving man and deplored his son's penchant for violence. Sacred Moon was merely seeking to avoid bloodshed when he forbade Blue Flower to see the white man.

The woman was surprised when Sacred Moon entered the lodge again, late that afternoon.

"Your white man has sent you a gift." He extended the brown coat toward her. "I accepted it for you with his word that he would not try to see you or the child again. He has gone now. He wishes you and the boy a good life." Sacred Moon left without waiting for a reply.

Blue Flower rubbed the soft woolen material against her cheek where a tear made its way down in spite of her efforts to control her emotions. She sat without moving for a long time, rubbing the garment against her face and remembering the past. The children were silent, sensing their mother's mood.

It was growing dark when she finally rose and slid her arms into the sleeves of the coat. She pulled the collar up around her face and knew the garment would keep her much warmer than her blankets did when the winds became fierce. Silently, she thanked Thornton McRae for remembering her in this way. She stuck her hands into the deep, warm pockets. That is when she discovered the embroidered bag. Thinking it to be another gift from Thornton McRae, she eagerly opened the drawstring top and pulled forth the contents, kneeling down and spilling them onto the blanket where she had been sitting.

Suddenly, she knew these were not meant for her. There was a letter in the white man's language, which she could not read. The paper was yellow and ragged around the edges. It was accompanied by a hand-painted photograph of a white woman and a man, perhaps of Blue Flower's age, but she could see that it was very old with tiny cracks crisscrossing each other. There was a small envelope, which she peeked into. It contained white man's money! Blue Flower could not be sure how much, but she felt it was a significant amount. Her heart beat quickly as she realized this was some other woman's coat which Thornton McRae had brought to her. Her curiosity was piqued by a small buckskin bag, which, like the other contents of the embroidered pouch, showed effects of age but also excellent handiwork. She fingered and inspected the bag before she opened it to examine the contents.

Reaching inside, Blue Flower grasped a strong buckskin thong. She withdrew it and drew a deep breath when she saw the amulet it held. It was a small cylindrical piece of cedar, perhaps three inches long, in the shape of a bear, an exquisite carving. She took the amulet closer to the door flap where the light was better to examine the figures that had been carved into the base and then etched as though by fire. Small figures, representing male and female, were shown dancing underneath evergreen boughs overhead. The Bear Dance—she knew it represented the Bear Dance, a ritual sacred to her people, held in the spring of each year. Tiny, perfectly proportioned dancers encircled the bear.

Bears were revered by her people, and she had seen similar representations many times. Sometimes they were wood carvings such as this, or perhaps exquisite beadwork on a medicine pouch or headband, but always they were possessed by some important member of the tribe, perhaps a medicine man or war chief. How had this amulet come to be in her hands? Where had Thornton McRae received this and what connection did it have with the other items—the letter, the picture, and the money? Where had the coat itself come from? Blue Flower was torn with emotion and terribly confused.

While Blue Flower pondered these questions, Little Eagle and Thorn Dove became restless and fretful. The woman raised herself from her musings, fed the children, and took them to her sister's lodge, where they always enjoyed playing with her young ones. Then she returned to her own tepee, closed the flap, and sat gently rubbing the small, exquisite carving, wishing she could have had just five minutes to speak with Thornton McRae.

Blue Flower was so occupied with her thoughts that she did not realize Night Wind had entered until he grabbed her hair. "What have you got, my white-loving Indian whore?" He flung her backward.

She lay silent where she fell and watched Night Wind grab the cedar carving.

"I was told the white man had been here, but did not

know you had seen him. Did he give you this?" Night Wind's voice seemed to whistle through his teeth as he waved the tiny bear before her.

"I did not see him. Your father brought me a gift from him. It is there." She motioned toward the coat. "The amulet was in the pocket," she added. "I do not know how it came to be there."

"First the white man steals our women; now he steals our tribal symbols. He must die! But first, we must find out where he stole the bear. Sacred Moon must be told of this!" He spat in her direction and left the lodge, taking the amulet with him.

Holding back tears, she sat up and brushed the hair from her face, determined that when Night Wind returned he would see no weakness in her.

Soon Night Wind rushed back inside, his eyes showing the fury inside him. He took up the coat and violently flung it toward her. "Wear this token of the white man, you lover of the whites! We must find your McRae!"

"I do not know where he is!"

"Lead us to where he might be camped!"

Night Wind's eyes showed blistering hatred, and Blue Flower was afraid. She put on the coat as he demanded. Then he extended the amulet toward her.

"Wear this! Maybe it will bring you good fortune in your search for McRae. If it fails, your life and your son's life will be sacrificed instead of his." His face was a mask of fury.

In fear, Blue Flower placed the thong over her head as Night Wind roughly led her outside, where he had left her horse saddled.

The Indian encampment was silent and seemingly deserted. No man wanted to be drawn into one of Night Wind's killing sprees except for the few who were his followers, those who assumed that at the old man's death Night Wind would replace his father as leader. As Night

Wind and Blue Flower rode through the circle of tepees, a few of Night Wind's loyal followers joined them.

Sacred Moon stepped from his lodge as they approached it at the west side of the village. Night Wind stopped his horse.

Though aged, Sacred Moon was still an impressive figure, forceful and stern. "My son, I caution you, do nothing foolish. I understand your anger and jealousy. Put them aside and bring the white man back. I, too, wish to know how he obtained the Bear Dance amulet."

Night Wind hesitated for a long moment before he answered. "I will honor your wishes for now, but someday soon I will kill Thornton McRae for desecrating my woman!"

"She was not your woman when he lived among us."

Sacred Moon's wise old eyes took in the crowd of horsemen who rode with Night Wind. There were ten of them, and he knew them to be vicious in their killing.

"My son, I forbid you to go with these men. You may take Blue Flower and seek McRae, but you must go alone with her. You seek to be in power among our people, then prove you are wise and capable. I am not long to be here. You have not much time to prove you are worthy of leadership. This is your chance to change many minds that have been turned against you by your own headstrong nature. Your men must stay here."

Night Wind considered momentarily. He knew his word would bring his men along with him or would bid them to follow the old man's words, for a while. He also knew that his father was right: many in the tribal council were reluctant to support him as leader.

"You are wise. I will do as you say. Blue Flower and I will go alone to seek the white man and to bring him back."

Blue Flower was relieved when the mounted Indians slowly turned and rode into the darkness toward their lodges. She could only hope that they would stay in the village rather than follow as soon as Sacred Moon slept.

She found McRae's camp easily. It was a favored spot in a shallow ravine where a thick grove of aspen stood. Just walking a horse through the aspen made the leaves quiver slightly, giving warning to a light sleeper. She knew he would hear their approach and called out before they got threateningly close.

"Thornton, don't shoot. It's Blue Flower."

From his bedroll, he had only to roll a yard or so to be protected behind a thick clump of young aspen. He was there long before he heard Blue Flower call.

"Are you alone, Blue Flower?" He knew the answer before he questioned.

"No, Night Wind is with me. But he has promised Sacred Moon your safety. We must talk to you."

"All right, come in to camp. But do it slow." He adjusted the hilt of his knife in its sheath so that it would be easily accessible. He knew well Night Wind's treacherous nature.

When they rode in close, Trap stood with his rifle in hand.

"Night Wind, drop your rifle before coming closer."

"I will not, white man!" Anger was apparent in his voice.

Blue Flower cringed inside, but spoke firmly. "We must do as he says. This is his camp, and it is the middle of the night."

"I will put down my rifle, white man, if you put yours down first."

Trap leaned his rifle against the nearest tree.

Night Wind slid his rifle gently to the ground.

"Come on in."

Trap could see that Blue Flower was wearing the coat he had left with Sacred Moon. The night air was chilly in spite of the season, and he was glad she wore the garment.

The two Indians rode forward.

When they grew close, the two stopped, and Blue Flower began an explanation for their midnight visit.

"Thornton, we are here to ask about this amulet that was inside the pocket of the coat you presented to Sacred Moon." She grasped the thong and pulled it forward in the scant moonlight.

"This is a symbol of the Bear Dance, which signifies good fortune and fertility among our people. Sacred Moon wishes for you to return to our village and tell him where you got the amulet."

Trap was completely puzzled. "Amulet? I don't know what you are talking about, Blue Flower."

Blue Flower hesitated a moment, then got to the part that was difficult for her to acknowledge. "Thornton, this coat has belonged to another woman. Who was she?" Feelings of jealousy stirred inside her.

Trap could hear pain in her voice, and he could not lie to her. "Blue Flower, I took the coat from a white woman who lived with me, but I have not took her as a wife." He repeated, "I don't know nothin' about any amulet."

"If you know nothing, white man, then you have no story to tell my father. I shall seek the white woman you speak of." Night Wind suddenly pulled his horse sideways to clear the aim of his hastily drawn knife.

He was not so quick that Trap did not anticipate the movement. Pulling his own knife as he lunged for the trees, Trap sent it spinning end over end. It plunged into Night Wind's chest at the same time Night Wind's knife embedded itself in a small aspen behind the spot where McRae had been standing.

As Night Wind toppled from his horse with a harsh, guttural sound, Blue Flower stuffed her fist into her mouth to stifle a cry. She watched Night Wind writhe on the ground for a few moments, then go limp. His horse stood over him, sniffing with curiosity, then paced away quickly at the smell of blood.

Turning toward McRae, Blue Flower could see he was unharmed as he came from the trees into the moon-dappled clearing. She flung herself off the horse and ran toward McRae, stepping around Night Wind's body in her race to the white man.

He extended his arms to catch her as she stumbled over the rough ground; he pulled her to him grateful for the feel of her in his arms and the fragrance of her hair against his cheek.

Pushing her away slightly so that he could look into her dark eyes, McRae brushed her face tenderly. "Blue Flower, are you all right?"

She knew she could not speak without tears, so she pulled her lips together in a tight smile and nodded.

"Do you know if you were followed here?" Trap knew the nature of Night Wind's companions and suspected that they were not too far behind.

"I do not know."

"We'd best figure you had some of Night Wind's bunch behind you. Let's clear out." He dragged Night Wind's body behind some bushes and concealed it as best he could in his haste while Blue Flower tried to gather in Night Wind's skittish stallion. At her approach, he pranced and reared, finally bounding swiftly back the way he had come.

As soon as Trap had his gear together, he pulled Blue Flower toward him for a quick embrace. "If anything happens to me, and you can't get back to Sacred Moon, go to my cabin at Elk Fork. Elizabeth is there. She is a good woman and will help you."

"Is this Elizabeth your new woman?"

"She's not my woman; you must understand that."

"Where are we going now?"

"We're heading in the direction of Elk Fork for now. Night Wind's men will probably turn back when we get close to the mines." Trap suddenly remembered the children. "Where are the boys? Sacred Moon told me about your youngest. That's why I agreed to leave without seeing you. I didn't want to interfere when it seemed your life was going well."

"They are with my sister and will be safe. Thornton, if we are pursued and must travel quickly, I am not sure if my horse can outrun theirs. If she cannot, you must go on without me. I know this country well and can find some place to hide."

"What are you saying? I can't do that! We have to stay together."

"No! You must listen to me! I know these men. I have grown up with them, and they will not harm me. It is you they hate. It will be worse if they know you killed Night Wind and took his woman. They want nothing from me!"

"They want blood, Blue Flower!"

"But not Ute blood. Thornton McRae, you must believe me. We are both safer apart if I cannot keep up." Her eyes were pleading.

"We'll see what happens" was the only acquiescence he could give to her plea although he realized there was logic in what she said.

Trap turned the packhorse loose, knowing he would follow, and they rode off hastily, keeping to a commonly used path, both for speed and so their prints would blend in with others recently made. They let their horses run, but stopped from time to time to listen for the beat of ponies on the trail behind them. At one such stop, Blue Flower laid her hand silently upon her lips in a quieting gesture. The expression on her face told McRae what she heard before she spoke.

"Riders, not far behind."

In the stillness of the night, McRae too could hear the far-off rumble of hooves pounding the trail. Kicking their horses hard, they began the race. Thornton McRae remembered Blue Flower's words well, and he glanced over his shoulder frequently to see if she was there.

Before they covered many miles, Blue Flower began to feel that her horse was tiring; her gait became uneven and awkward. She remembered a small trail that led off to the right not far ahead. Hoping the horsemen were not close enough to see her turn off, she slowed, gave a final glance at McRae, and headed her pony up a tiny deer trail. Pointing the mare into the brush, she bounded off and quieted the animal with soft touches as Night Wind's warriors raced past, just minutes behind McRae. She prayed that McRae's big gelding would hold out. Together, she and McRae would likely both have died. Separately, there was a chance for each, or with luck perhaps both, of them.

Drawing a long breath, Blue Flower tried to decide what her next step should be. She was sorely tempted to return to her own lodge and her sons. But fear made her consider her actions very carefully. She was not as confident as she had tried to sound to McRae that she was safe from Night Wind's vengeful followers. As the warriors had sped by, she had tried to determine their number. Although she could not be sure, it had sounded as if there were no more than five or six horses, which meant there were others of his close-knit band left behind, whether in the village or on the trail she could not venture to guess.

Blue Flower knew the way to Elk Fork and remembered the approximate location of McRae's cabin. She did not intend to seek help from McRae's white woman, but if she could get close to Elk Fork, perhaps she could find Thornton McRae. Setting out, she made her way as closely as she could in a direction parallel with the trail Thornton and the Ute riders had taken, yet keeping to the shelter of the trees.

CHAPTER 15

IT WAS ALMOST sunup when Blue Flower heard the first rifle shots. She was in a shallow canyon and had been wondering for some time if she was lost. When the shots sounded, Blue Flower quickly drew the mare back into a shroud of trees and listened. Shots were coming from a ridge slightly to the left and were being returned from a point down a small gorge to her right. Her position was perilous because of the rocks surrounding her little shelter of trees. There were numerous points from which bullets could ricochet. Pulling her horse into the shelter of the pines, she dismounted and drew herself up into as small a target as she could manage and lay among the thick tree trunks.

Soon a big volley of shots echoed through the small canyon, and Blue Flower's horse went down with blood pumping from her chest. The mare groaned and grunted with pain as her legs threshed about. Terrified that the horse's death throes might reveal her hiding place, Blue Flower rose to a crouch and slipped a knife from underneath her blouse where she always kept it tucked into the band of her skirt. With a swift thrust, she severed the suffering animal's trachea and listened with heartbreak as the last breath whistled through the mare's throat.

Looking desperately for a more protected shelter, she sighted a rock ledge about twenty feet away with a small overhang. Crawling and half rolling, she made her way toward the protection of the tiny cavity. Gaining the shelter of the ledge, she crawled underneath and pulled some small rocks into a mound in front of her for additional protection. She lay breathlessly for a few minutes listening to the shots being fired, trying unsuccessfully to identify the number of firearms being used and wondering if McRae was being fired upon.

Finally, Blue Flower put her hand down in front of her in order to thrust her body farther back into the protection of the rocky overhang. As she pushed herself backward, her hand slipped in moisture. Looking down, she saw a dark stain on the rock in front of her. Her right hand was red when she turned the palm upward. For the first time, she felt a slight pain in her side. She put her hand underneath her blouse, which was now growing wet with blood, and felt a small puckering of wet flesh on the left near the base of her rib cage. Twisting slightly to accommodate the movement of her right arm, Blue Flower reached behind her and felt to the left side of her back. The feel of warm blood gave her relief. The bullet, obviously of a small caliber, had penetrated her body and was not trapped inside in some organ. She settled herself as comfortably as possible to wait for the firing to end, hoping that the bleeding would soon cease.

The firing soon grew more distant, moving gradually to the west and becoming intermittent. Finally, it faded away altogether. Blue Flower continued to lie in the shade of the rock throughout the day as flies began to buzz around the carcass of her pony. She was sick at heart and wondered if she would ever see her babies or Thornton McRae again. From time to time, she fingered the cedar amulet, which she still wore around her neck, and wondered if it brought a curse. Her life had certainly begun to fall apart from the moment the token had come into her possession.

By late afternoon, the bleeding had almost stopped; Blue Flower crept out from her tiny shelter and stood up, feeling light-headed because she had not eaten in almost twenty-four hours. From the carcass of the horse, she retrieved her coat and her buffalo-bladder water bag, gave the pony a final pat, and began walking down the canyon.

Slowly she made her way toward Elk Fork, keeping to the trees and gullies, seeking berries along the way with which to keep up her strength. Finding water became a bigger problem than she had anticipated. The end of summer was arriving, which meant that the frequent afternoon thundershowers had ceased. The days were still hot, and the earth soaked up what moisture was around. Here and there she found tiny pools. By digging the mud away, she usually found enough silt-laden water to quench her thirst, but never enough to completely fill her water bag.

It was not much more than a good day's walk to Elk Fork from where her horse had fallen, but Blue Flower did not have a good day. All night she walked, stopping frequently because of the pain in her ribs and shivering in spite of the warmth of the coat.

When the first light of day arrived, she looked around her, examining the countryside. The peaks that had surrounded her hiding place of the day before were behind her, but only slightly. She walked a little farther, finally coming upon what she knew was usually a fast-running stream. Today, it was slow and meandering around the stones that filled the shallow gully. Finding the deepest point, she drank for several moments, dipping her flushed face into the cool water, which ran around a large stone and formed a pool. Then she filled her water bag.

Having rested awhile in the shade of the brush along the creek, she gained the energy to cleanse her wound. Without a receptacle in which to heat water, she could only wash the dried blood away carefully with a square torn from her skirt, dampened with the cold water from the languid stream. Blue Flower knew she was becoming feverish, but so far there was no outward sign of infection. Folding the square that she had used for bathing the wound, she rewrapped it with a wide swath of fabric torn from her skirt, binding the layers of material closely to absorb as much of the blood as possible. Then she crept into a deep stand of brush to sleep.

Voices and the snorting and stamping of horses awoke her when the sun was but halfway across the sky. She lay on her back and did not move, angry at herself for not having heard the approach of the men. She could only hope she was deeply hidden enough that she would not be seen.

Someone spoke from near the stream, "That there's a moccasin print!"

Blue Flower held her breath, cursing herself for leaving one moccasin print. She had been careful to try when possible to step only on stones and to leave no trail to her hiding place in the bushes.

There came a blustering answer, "Yep, it might be. But it's a few hours old. Kinda little. We ain't skeered of no Indian that little."

There were guffaws as the men filled their canteens, watered their horses, and moved on quickly. From the sounds, Blue Flower judged they might number perhaps a half dozen.

The Indian woman lay where she was until the late afternoon sun had dipped behind a mountain. Then she slipped down to the rocks beside the stream and unbound her makeshift bandage. Then she bent forward painfully, straightened up, and examined the wound. What she had feared was there, a tiny white ooze of pus forced outward by her bending. There were several native herbs that would help to stop the infection, but she had seen none of them since being wounded.

After rebandaging her midsection, she got up and pushed on slowly, trying to remember the way to Thornton McRae's cabin and hoping intensely that she would meet him along the way. If she did not, she planned to hide nearby and wait for him to return to the cabin. She had her doubts that McRae's white woman would be as hospitable as he had indicated.

As Blue Flower drew nearer to the mining area round Elk Fork, she found the berries that had been keeping her alive becoming scarce, the bushes having been picked over recently in most places. A time or two she heard shots far off and wondered if the renegade Ute were responsible. Fearfully, she traveled almost totally by darkness, knowing this would make it much more unlikely that she would encounter McRae should he be nearby. But her fear of being found alone by the wrong men was strong. The pain in her side grew worse, and she had to clean the wound more frequently, washing her bandages carefully in a stream when she found one. Angry red fingers branched out from the pus-filled pocket, and Blue Flower frequently shivered and alternately sweltered from a fever that was growing worse.

And thus, Blue Flower doggedly made her way around the village of Elk Fork and collapsed but a few miles from Thornton McRae's cabin.

CHAPTER 16

WHEN BLUE FLOWER's tale was finished, Elizabeth sat in silence for a long time. Deck and Blue Flower wondered what her reaction would be to the reality that the woman she had assisted was actually her husband's other wife. They were both surprised by her first comment.

"Then Thornton McRae is a good man. At first I had suspected it was so, then had second thoughts. He certainly never gave me much in the way to judge him."

Blue Flower expressed her bewilderment. "But you are his wife. Why do you question if he was a good man?"

It was Elizabeth's turn to tell her Thornton McRae story. When she finished, she declared simply, "You, Blue Flower, are his wife."

As the stories the two women told had grown more complicated, Deck had withdrawn to a far corner of their dark chamber, but he listened intently, sometimes frowning in his attempt to understand the full meaning of these women's experience with a man he had known off and on since he was a child. He struggled to intertwine what the women related to what he knew of Trap McRae. When the women grew silent after their stories had been told, he spoke up.

"Seems I ought to get busy and see if I can find ole Trap."

Elizabeth moved to the mouth of the cave to stir the fire and place a pot of water on it. "That's probably a good idea, Deck. And, first of all, find Sheriff Barnes. Maybe tomorrow, if all seems to be going well here." She was reluctant to have Deck leave, although she knew they needed the help of the sheriff.

Blue Flower could no longer repress the question that plagued her: "How did you get the amulet, Elizabeth?"

Elizabeth knelt on the stones before the fire and poked at it with a stick. "My mother got it from an Indian man she and my father had befriended. It's all told in the letter that you found in the coat pocket. Let me read some of that letter to you."

Elizabeth had left the embroidered bag and its contents deep within the coat pocket when the three of them made their exodus from the cabin, thinking it was as safe a place as she could think of. Now she removed the letter and straightened the yellow paper, moving to the front of the cave where light was good.

Deck busied himself cutting up a rabbit he had snared earlier in the morning; he placed the parts in the pot that Elizabeth had put on the fire and added a few herbs that he had found near the spring.

Elizabeth wrapped her skirts around her and sat down on the edge of the blanket where Blue Flower lay, motioning for Deck to come closer.

"This was written to my grandmother shortly after my brother was born. It was to announce his birth to the grandparents, and it was the last letter my mother ever wrote."

During the time of my expectancy, which has been very difficult indeed, another unexpected challenge arose quite by accident. While Edward was out hunting, he found sign of a grizzly bear; they are huge animals whose size and ferociousness far exceed that of two or three of the black bears to which you are accustomed. While trying to avoid an encounter with the bear, an endeavor in which he succeeded, he did find a victim of the beast. Near a stream where Edward sought to obtain water for himself and his horse, he ran across an Indian who had been badly mangled by the animal. He was lying underneath some trees nearby, and it appeared that his scalp had been almost ripped away. Also, flesh had been torn from his chest and back, and the bone of his right leg could be seen where the meat had been shredded down almost to his knee.

What decision could poor Edward make except to bring the unfortunate man home, draped across his saddle, a savage thing to have to do to a brutally injured person? But there was no other way to bring him here where we could nurse him. The Indian responded for a few days to the best treatment we could give, which, as you can suppose, was somewhat feeble, since we had no surgeon to treat injuries of that extent.

Contrary to what you hear said about the red man from your Boston newspapers, our patient was a very gracious man who spoke a few words of English. Since Edward can speak a few words in the language of various Indian tribes, we were able to communicate somewhat. As best we could understand, his name was some kind of owl, and he was a leader among his people, a chief, I suppose. He was on some kind of spiritual mission, which is why he came to be in the forest alone.

Anyway, to shorten the story, he died soon thereafter in spite of our best efforts, but blessed my then unborn child by giving me a cedar amulet that he wore about his neck and which is charmingly adorned with figures of bears and dancing Indians. It is quite beautiful. In all honesty, the Indian seemed quite serious when he told me that the spirits would bless my child through this necklace, or amulet as he seemed to call it, if I would promise to return it to his people. Of course, I promised to try to do so. And I shall try, although I would be just as happy if I should never see any of his people again, for they have been known to commit atrocities in spite of Chief Owl's gracious manner.

However, the child has been born a healthy infant in spite of the fact that I feared it would be stillborn, and I often wondered if I would perish as well, since I have been so infirm for the last few months. Perhaps the chief's necklace did bring the good will of God to little Frederick, but I suspect it was the capable ministrations of Mrs. Murphy who delivered our tiny gift of happiness.

Elizabeth folded the worn pages. "My mother prized the cedar bear. I can remember how she smiled when she talked about the Indian's blessing, and I thought then that's why she was so fond of it. Now, I suppose it was because it is so exquisitely carved, and my mother had little in the way of jewelry or ornaments for our home. I remember, too, that I was charmed by it and loved to hold it and have daydreams about the Indian figures although some of the thoughts were frightening. As I grew older, I thought about it less and less and eventually sort of forgot about it. I was surprised when my grandmother put this packet together in the embroidered bag and presented it to me on my sixteenth birthday."

Blue Flower said nothing, silently remembering the stories about the disappearance of Chief Crested Owl many years ago, after he had slain his brother Hooded Hawk.

Deck rode out before daylight the next morning on Pete, having refused the offer of Elizabeth's horse; he explained that it was best he travel as he usually did in case he encountered suspicious Indians. He and Elizabeth agreed that his first goal was to locate Sheriff Red Barnes and obtain his assistance in assuring the safety of the three of them in returning to Elizabeth's cabin or at least to Elk Fork. The search for Thornton McRae could wait.

The day dragged on; Elizabeth paced back and forth both inside and outside the cave to relieve her anxiety. Midafternoon brought rumblings in the mountains, with thunder seeming to roll from peak to peak. Elizabeth had difficulty remaining inside their shelter; the lightning flashes, bright and furious, seemed to draw her outside to watch. She hoped the afternoon storm would bring rain, since the little spring nearby was barely supplying enough water for their needs.

It was late afternoon when Elizabeth caught the smell of smoke drifting through the air. She was at the spring, filling their water vessels and feeling dejected because the storm had passed without dropping any rain. Looking up, she saw smoke rising lazily toward the sky, west of where she was. When her eyes finally adjusted to the glare of the afternoon sun, she could see the flames high atop the ridge to the west. Transfixed, she watched as the fire began in minutes to eat its way down the steep slope, devouring the dry timber in its path. Although the fire was miles away, a brisk wind from the west was pushing the thick smoke ahead of it and, Elizabeth feared, was driving the fire in their direction. Elizabeth sprang into action, grabbing the water vessels and rushing down the hillside.

"Blue Flower, the lightning has started a forest fire up on the ridge! It's still a long way off, but headed this way! We must do something!"

Blue Flower looked startled as Elizabeth ran shouting into the cave.

"Help me up, Elizabeth. Let me look."

With Elizabeth's help, Blue Flower made her way outside and stood watching the flames licking their way through the trees.

"We must do something!" Elizabeth repeated. "We must leave!"

Blue Flower spoke calmly. "Where could we go that we know would be safe for us? It is better to stay here." She knew their primary threat was not the fire itself, but the smoke filling their shelter.

"The cave faces south, Elizabeth, and the smoke is coming from the west. But we still should figure out some way to hang a blanket over the entrance in case the wind should bring the fire and smoke in this direction." She paused for a moment.

"I know what we can do. I'm only sorry that I am not able to help you with the work, but you must take the hatchet that Deck left us and cut two saplings." She turned and leaned on Elizabeth's arm as she went back inside. "We must have two saplings strong enough so that we can wedge both ends of a blanket up against each side of the entrance. See"—she pointed to the rocky inside walls—"we can wedge a strong young tree trunk up under one of the rocks and into the floor. One on either side will hold up a blanket across the entrance and keep the smoke out."

The plan made sense to Elizabeth. Climbing the steep incline above the cave, Elizabeth searched for two young trees of the right size. They were not difficult to locate, and cutting them took only a short time. She dragged them down the slope, one at a time. Soon, the two women were judging carefully the length to which the trees should be cut. Before long, they were ready to put up the make-shift door if the smoke made it necessary.

Elizabeth built a fire outside, confident that she did not have to worry about the smoke being seen. As she prepared their meal, she searched the darkening sky, examining each cloud for its promise of rain and finding little to encourage her.

As they ate, Elizabeth asked Blue Flower a question that had been on her mind since she had first heard Blue Flower speak.

"May I ask you how you learned to speak such perfect English? Certainly not from Thornton McRae."

"I learned most of it from a white woman who was brought into our camp maybe five years ago. Some of the young braves had snatched her from a wagon train out on the prairie. They brought her into camp, arguing over whose squaw she would become. Sacred Moon settled that question. As our leader, he took over and claimed her for his squaw. Actually, she was not, but it kept the young braves from her. She taught many of us to speak your language. The woman earned the respect of our people, so one day Sacred Moon rode away with her and took her back to a white village, releasing her near enough to the white people that she could ride in safely. We learned much of the white man from her."

There was another question that had been burning in Elizabeth's mind. "The men of your village—I have heard—they sometimes have more than one wife?" Elizabeth stammered because to her the subject was a delicate one and she did not wish to sound as if she were accusing the men of Blue Flower's village of wrongdoing.

"Yes, some of them do. It is not unusual for one man to have two wives, particularly if they are sisters."

Elizabeth finally thought she understood why Blue Flower had shown no sign of resentment toward her as Thornton McRae's legal wife.

While cleaning their plates, Elizabeth quietly watched the flames: the growing fire developed a second arm that took off into a new direction, eating southward as the wind whipped it. She could tell that access from Elk Fork might soon be cut off completely, eliminating the possibility that Deck would return to them that night. With anxiety, she went back inside to tell Blue Flower of the new direction the fire was taking.

"There is no need to worry. We will be safe. We must let in fresh air while we can and we will take turns watching so we will know when the smoke gets too thick. You sleep first. My side pains me, and I must be very tired before I can sleep. We must take one more precaution. Build up the fire outside so it will burn for quite a while, and bring the rest of the wood inside with enough coals from the evening fire to last through the night. Put the coals in the heavy iron skillet and cover them with a heavy layer of ash."

Elizabeth asked no questions; Blue Flower's directions seemed to have purpose. After these preparations had been made, Elizabeth wrapped herself in the extra blanket and fell into a light sleep. She awoke reluctantly when Blue Flower called her.

"You were sleeping soundly, and I hate to wake you, but it is time to spread the blanket over the entrance."

Elizabeth coughed softly and agreed. Their shelter was not totally dark, but had a dim, rosy hue from the combination of smoke-filtered moonlight and the eerie brightness that the forest fire cast across the night sky. Elizabeth took a quick look around outside and was awed by the immensity of the flames moving rapidly through the darkness. She did not voice her fear to Blue Flower but felt that the Indian woman probably could sense it.

The two hoisted one end of the blanket, speared it on the sharpened end of the first sapling, and wedged it in place beneath a small, rocky abutment on the left side of the entrance. They did the same on the right side. Blue Flower moved stiffly, but her agility was slowly returning.

Holding the blanket flap to one side at the right lower corner, Blue Flower asked Elizabeth to bring the coals and build a small fire at the corner.

"We will have some light inside, Elizabeth, and it will also keep the wild animals away." She tied a knot in the corner of the blanket, leaving a small opening through which their fire could breathe.

Elizabeth was not sure she wanted to ask about the wild animals that Blue Flower had so casually mentioned, but she finally decided it best to do so.

"Wild animals?"

"This place has been the den for many an animal. Can you not smell the musty odors left behind? And when Deck first brought Millie in, couldn't you see her nervousness when she was placed at the back of the cave where, no doubt, many bears have slept through the winter." She suddenly realized that Elizabeth had no familiarity with these things that were so commonplace to Blue Flower. She softened her comments. . . .

"I was just concerned that the forest fire might drive them to seek shelter inside here, but there's no need to worry now. If anything dares to come close, the fire you built outside will keep the animal at bay; if anything gets too close, the horse will let us know. Just keep the fire in here burning low and steady and wake me if you hear anything." Within moments, Blue Flower was snoring steadily.

Elizabeth tried to adopt Blue Flower's confidence in their safety, and it was not as difficult as she had expected. The soft light from the low fire and the occasional shuffling of the horse became strangely comforting.

Elizabeth wasn't sure if she had been dozing when Millie's shrill neigh brought her up in alarm. Blue Flower awakened at the same time.

"Elizabeth, what is it?" she whispered.

"I don't know. I haven't heard anything." She stared at the blanket, which was swaying slightly.

Blue Flower was rising and half crawling over the floor toward Elizabeth. The horse stomped and neighed. She spoke gently to the horse, then to Elizabeth. "Take a stick and roll out one of the burning coals. That will attract the attention of anything that's out there. Then ease back the edge of the blanket and see what's there. Have your rifle ready." Now she made no effort to keep her voice down, knowing that sounds would likely intimidate most animals.

With trepidation, Elizabeth did as Blue Flower said. With a stick of firewood, she pushed one of the largest coals underneath the blanket, then quickly moved to the right and peered outside the edge of the makeshift door. At first she saw only a pink-tinged blackness. Then there were two yellow sparks of light. Quickly, she realized she was looking into the eyes of some animal as its focus moved up from the rolling coal of fire to her face. Elizabeth froze as the eyes seemed to drill in on her. She jerked the rifle up, thankful that Deck had left it ready to fire. Her quick movement must have startled the animal because the eyes disappeared in a flash before she could get the rifle in a position to fire.

Blue Flower responded at once when she saw Elizabeth lower the rifle, "Elizabeth, our fire outside must have been too small." She did not point out that the blaze had gone out while Elizabeth dozed. "Let's put a fire barrier a little farther out, between the boulder and the side of the mountain. We do not need a large blaze, but we must keep it going all night."

Elizabeth was slow to react, "What do you suppose was out there?" Fear choked her voice, constricting her throat muscles.

"Only a wolf or mountain lion. Did you not see anything?"

"All I could see were the eyes!" Elizabeth could not stop the shudder that shook her body.

Elizabeth started to stack the wood a little ways from the cave, with Blue Flower helping as best she could. When the fire was lighted, Elizabeth and Blue Flower went back inside and sat down in exhaustion near the entrance to the cave. Blue Flower had dragged her blanket closer to the entrance and lay with her face near the makeshift door.

Elizabeth clutched her rifle and tried to relax. She knew that any further sleep was probably impossible for either of them. Elizabeth lost track of time and did not know if it was one hour or several hours later when she felt Blue Flower's hand touch her wrist softly. The Indian woman motioned for Elizabeth to peer outside.

Putting her face close to Blue Flower's, she pulled the blanket aside an inch or so. She almost cried out, but instead covered her mouth with her hand. She could discern a figure standing tall above the low blaze of the fire they had set. It was obvious that the figure was that of an Indian dressed in frayed buckskins. She jerked the flap of the blanket closed.

"What shall we do?" Her fear was greater than when she had stared into the glowing eyes of the animal.

"We must not show fear. We must invite him inside," Blue Flower whispered.

"How do we know he is alone?" Elizabeth countered.

"We don't know. You take the rifle and sit there in the shadows." She motioned toward Millie's corner. Then she rose stiffly and pulled back the blanket.

Elizabeth could see from the tiny flames of their fire that their visitor was old. As he stepped into the cavern, the light from below seemed to pull the wrinkles in his face downward and deepen them into gullies along his cheeks. Blue Flower spoke to him with respect, gesturing toward Elizabeth. The old man nodded politely toward Elizabeth; she nodded back, feeling her fear subside a little. Surely the old man did not bring harm. Blue Flower stirred the small flames of their fire, warming coffee and food for their guest as she talked with him in a language Elizabeth could not understand. A weight of weariness seemed to fall upon Elizabeth. Pillowing her head and shoulders against Millie's saddle, she watched Blue Flower and the old man talk in the strange language until her eyelids grew heavy and closed.

Elizabeth awoke with a start the next morning, sitting up quickly and wondering what had awakened her. She reached for her rifle before she realized that it had only been a gentle nudge from Millie that brought her from her sleep. The events of the night thundered into her mind, bringing the realization that she had not been dreaming. A nightmarish reality set in as she peered throughout the gloomy interior of the cavern, seeking Blue Flower and their aged visitor. No one was to be seen, but there was a bit of daylight creeping in from the edges of the blanket that still hung over the entryway. The bit of brightness brought her fully awake, and she sprang up and ran to the doorway with a hungry Millie following. Pulling the blanket to one side, she could see that sunlight was making a feeble path through the heavy smoke that still hung outside. Still somewhat disoriented, she stood rubbing her shoulder where it had rested too heavily against the saddle and peered to her left to see how far the sun had risen above the mountains. It was just clearing the eastern peaks. Though the skies were still a murky brown, the air outside seemed almost fresh and cool after the stale smell of the cave.

Millie found a few clumps of grass nearby and began to graze while Elizabeth looked around at the smoldering landscape. Although the fire had left their little area of the mountain untouched, as far as she could see the mountainsides were blackened. Spires of scorched tree trunks stood starkly among piles of ash, still smoking here and there. In the direction of Elk Fork, fresh smoke still billowed. The fire had not come closer than perhaps a hundred yards from their refuge, since brush was sparse on this part of the mountain.

Now that she realized the worst was over, Elizabeth's fears seemed to dissipate and she began looking for Blue Flower. She found the Indian woman kneeling on the ground beside the spring. Blue Flower did not look up as Elizabeth approached. With dismay, Elizabeth saw that ashes and soot floated heavily on the small pool.

"Our water supply is ruined!" She moaned.

At her words, Blue Flower stirred. "We can dip off the worst of it, and the underground water will freshen it within a few hours." As she spoke she began to skim off the top of the water, using her cupped palms.

Elizabeth followed Blue Flower's example.

"You seem stronger this morning."

"I am much better."

"Where is our visitor, the old man?"

"He is gone," Blue Flower replied shortly. Flicking off the worst of the scum from the top of the water, she gathered a small amount into her left palm and splashed it on her face.

"Who was he? You seemed to know him." Elizabeth likewise dipped her palm into the water and bathed her face.

"I know of him. I never knew him. Please, we must not

speak of him again." She sat very still, with her head tucked against her chest.

"I do not understand. Did you have some disagreement?" There was a puzzled look on Elizabeth's face as she dried it on the hem of her dress.

Rising and shaking the dust and ash from her skirt, Blue Flower spoke resolutely. "You do not understand our customs. I must tell you that I gave him the amulet. I took it from your coat pocket and gave it to him. Now, let's speak no more of him or the amulet."

"All right, we will say no more, but I'm glad you gave him the amulet. I was beginning to think it was a curse anyway."

Blue Flower suddenly turned and ran back down the trail toward the cave.

Elizabeth deliberately stayed away for a while, pondering the brief comments Blue Flower had made and giving the Indian woman some time alone. When she returned, Blue Flower was frying bacon with a thoughtful look on her face, so Elizabeth did not speak.

Soon Blue Flower looked up from where she was turning the strips of frying meat. "We must go back now."

"Go back?" Elizabeth queried.

"Yes, we must go back to your cabin; perhaps you can get into town. I must go home!"

"What are you saying? We must wait for Deck and Sheriff Barnes."

"No! There is evil here, I feel it! I smell it! We must go!"

In spite of her recent assurances to speak no more of their visitor, Elizabeth confronted her. "It's the old man, isn't it? He told you something that frightened you. You must tell me who he is!"

For the first time that morning, Blue Flower raised her head and met Elizabeth's eyes. Her face was somber with an expression akin to fear. "All right. His name is Hooded Hawk, and he is one of our ancient ones. Now, let's discuss it no more. We must prepare to leave."

"We don't know the way back. Nor do we know if we can get around the fire that seems to be still burning back that way." Her protests were expressed weakly; she felt overwhelmed by Blue Flower's sudden show of stubborn will.

"I can find the way! I cannot stay here another night, no matter what!"

Suddenly, remembering the terror of the previous night, Elizabeth made up her mind to follow Blue Flower's bidding. Stashing most of their supplies in the back of the cave, they tied their small amount of remaining food, a water bag, one blanket, and the coat onto Millie's saddle and set out, leading the horse and sliding down the steep slope away from the cave.

CHAPTER 17

IT WAS A far different landscape through which they rode than when Deck led them to the cave. Blue Flower gave Millie a sense of direction and then let her pick her way through the still smoldering trees and around piles of hot ash. The day was warm and dry. Ashes clung to Millie's mane and tail; Elizabeth and Blue Flower looked gray-haired before they had traveled far. They rode downslope and a little to the east of the route they had traveled with Deck; here the fire had not destroyed the vegetation so thoroughly. Elizabeth could tell that they were traveling in a southerly direction that would eventually bring them near Elk Fork, and she felt renewed confidence in Blue Flower's ability to guide them home. Still she kept looking ahead and watching the ridges, hoping to see Deck and Pete appear somewhere on the parched landscape.

By midafternoon, the slowly traveling women approached Wolf Point. They veered to the right in order to take advantage of the opportunity the great promontory offered to survey the countryside around. Leaving Blue Flower and Millie to rest, Elizabeth climbed the huge, sloping rock. Peering southward, she could see with relief that the fire had not traveled so far to the southeast as to reach her place, but had been halted by a wide, dry creek bed. She vaguely remembered having crossed it during their midnight ride. The forest below was green and alive again. Elizabeth could see far-off grazing animals that had been prematurely pushed out of the high country, before their usual fall departure to lower elevations. The sky to the west was the color of a late-summer persimmon. Above her and to the east, the brown haze was barely noticeable.

It was almost dark when they reached Elizabeth's place. They approached stealthily through the trees, having tied the horse farther back in the forest. When they came in sight of the cabin, they could see the door was standing open. For a few moments, the women stayed in the shadows and merely watched for any movement or other sign of human presence.

Finally Elizabeth whispered, "I think it's all right. I'm going in." She gave the rifle to Blue Flower. "It is ready to shoot. If something happens, use it." Then she showed Blue Flower how to fill the chamber with another round of ammunition.

Elizabeth darted across the clearing to the nearest corner of the cabin. Pausing and listening briefly, she heard nothing and began to creep slowly toward the open door, her back pressed against the outside walls. She peered into the window beside the door and saw no one, so she boldly stepped onto the porch and went inside.

The place was a mess, with everything pulled out of the cupboards and her closet; even the thin mattress had been dumped from the bed onto the floor. Even so, Elizabeth felt fortunate: she had left behind nothing of value except for a small amount of food.

Elizabeth motioned for the exhausted Indian woman to come inside, then returned to the forest for Millie. The horse shed had been turned inside out, just as the house had been. Anything of possible use had been taken, and the small bag of oats that Elizabeth kept for an occasional treat for Millie was gone. After the horse had been unsaddled, brushed down, and watered, she staked the mare out near the house so she could safely graze for a while, then turned to go inside.

It was then she noticed the amulet, hanging from its thin leather thong. She uttered a short, stifled cry, which brought Blue Flower to the door. Elizabeth pointed wordlessly.

As usual, Blue Flower spoke in a calm, emotionless voice. "I saw it when we first approached. While you were caring for the horse, I took a closer look. You think it is cursed, but any curse that might have been associated with it is gone. It has been blessed." She gestured toward the cedar figurine. "You see, it is covered with ash—"

"Of course it's covered with ash!" Elizabeth interrupted. "You're covered with ash! I'm covered with ash, but we surely have not been blessed! Quite the opposite, if you ask me! I'm cutting that thing down and burning it! How in the world did it get here?" She started toward the door to get a knife.

Blue Flower caught Elizabeth's forearms as she tried to rush by. Her grip was strong for a woman so recently weakened by fever. Her eyes were like ebony as she gently shook Elizabeth.

"Let me finish. If you look closely, you will see tiny droplets of blood seeping from the eyes of the bear."

"Blood? You mean it's got blood on it, too?" The strain of the last few days had Elizabeth frenzied. "What kind of blood?"

"Who knows? It may be the blood of a rabbit, a human, or maybe of the bear itself. I do not know. It is said it weeps tears of its own blood. It has been blessed and left here as a sign of safety for us. You cannot destroy it!"

"I can, and I will. This is my house, not yours!" She struggled to free herself from Blue Flower's grasp.

"Elizabeth, listen to me! Ashes represent purification. This figure has had the ash stroked into the textures of the wood itself. It is no accident that it is covered with ash. Also, the legends that accompany this and many other tribal symbols speak of those who are capable of producing their own tears of blood. I do not know that they are true, but I do not know that they are not true. I have always suspected that a human supplied the blood in tears in order to make their own medicine, their spiritual strength, seem greater. I do not know. But you must not destroy it!"

Elizabeth slowly forced herself to turn her head and look toward the hanging amulet. Indeed, below the eyes there were tiny black smudges that could have been blood or some other dark substance. She knew she could not let herself get caught up in Indian lore, but had to regain control of herself, her home. She shook herself free from Blue Flower's grip and raced inside. Standing in the familiar surroundings of the kitchen, she began to get control of her fears. She started a fire and began rummaging for food, seeking something that the intruders might have left. There was half a loaf of stale bread from which she trimmed a few spots of blue mold. Deep in the back of a lower shelf was a jar of Betsy's plum jelly that had been overlooked. She put a few spoonfuls of coffee, left in a tin can that had been labeled "Lard," in the battered pot and whisked out the door with the water bucket.

When she had the coffeepot boiling, she felt calm enough to address Blue Flower. "I see no choice but to stay here tonight, even with that wretched thing hanging outside. But as soon as daylight comes, we are going to Elk Fork, even if we have to fight off that gang of ruffians ourselves. They've probably cleared out of the country. We've got to get to Sheriff Barnes to see what's going on and to find out what has happened to Deck!"

"And we must try to find out what has happened to McRae," Blue Flower said softly.

"Yes, that too, I guess," Elizabeth replied after a pause.

As they finished cleaning the kitchen and prepared for bed, Elizabeth asked, "I don't guess it would do any good for me to ask you more about that hideous bear and the old man."

"No, it would not," Blue Flower responded.

Almost angrily, Elizabeth grabbed her blanket and retired to the small living-room sofa, leaving the bed for her guest.

CHAPTER 18

THE TWO WOMEN were barely out of their little lane on the way to town the next morning when Blue Flower touched Elizabeth's shoulder.

"I hear horses coming."

Elizabeth saw a thick patch of scrub oak, and she pulled the horse behind it. Soon the riders came into view. The first thing Elizabeth recognized was Pete, ambling along as if time stood still. Deck was astride him with his floppy-brimmed hat askew as always. Beside him was a tall, square-shouldered man, whom Elizabeth thought was Sheriff Barnes. She kept Millie still until she could be sure who rode with Deck, but soon enough she could see a shock of red hair spilling from underneath the big gray hat the man wore, and she could see the sun brightening the star on his chest. She urged Millie forward.

The two men stopped short at the sight of the horse emerging from the brush some thirty yards up the road from them.

When Deck recognized the women, he hurried Pete as much as possible by flogging the mule's hindquarters with his hat.

"Miss Elizabeth! Miss Elizabeth! What are you doin' here? We was comin' after you!"

He jumped off Pete and made the final few yards more quickly than the mule. He reached up his left hand and grabbed Elizabeth's right. She thought for a startled moment that he was going to kiss it, but he merely took it and rubbed it up and down his stubbled cheek.

Elizabeth smiled with as much pleasure as Deck showed,

and Blue Flower slipped off the back of the horse to stand beside Deck. "Deck, you've been hurt!" She said.

Deck's right arm was in a sling, folded across his chest.

"Wal, don't worry none 'bout that. 'Tain't nothin' like yore wound was."

Sheriff Barnes rode up. "Mornin'. Don't let Deck short-sell that injury of his. I don't think he ought to be out to-day, but he was so concerned about the two of you even Betsy couldn't keep him from comin' along. Glad to see you're all right."

Deck was almost blushing from the attention, so he changed the subject. "We brung you some grub. I figgered if we found you up at the cave, you'd be sorta gettin' hungry by now."

"You're right, we've had some skimpy meals the last couple of days," Elizabeth said. "Let's get back up to the cabin. You can tell us what's been going on while I cook some of that food."

Elizabeth noticed that Blue Flower was staring at the ground, her pleasure at seeing Deck and Sheriff Barnes dampened. She knew she had to ask the question that was on Blue Flower's mind.

"What about Thornton McRae? Do you know where he is?"

"We're not sure. Since we ain't seen him, I've an idea that he might have gone back to Sacred Moon's camp, maybe to see about his son." Red Barnes seemed embarrassed by the subject.

"He would not do that, without knowing if I was safe or not!" The words seemed to burst from Blue Flower's mouth. She glanced timidly at Elizabeth.

Elizabeth could see that she regretted her outburst. "It's all right, Blue Flower. Let's get back now and find out all the news on a full stomach." Elizabeth reached her hand down to help Blue Flower up onto the horse.

As soon as they rode up to the cabin, Deck spied the

small cedar amulet dangling from the porch post. He stopped Pete shortly and sat staring at it. "What's that danged thang doin' there?" he asked with a bit of nervousness in his voice.

"We'll tell you our stories, Deck, after you've told us yours," Elizabeth said, dismounting. "Sheriff Barnes, the house was raided while we were away. It seems nothing was taken except food, and a few odds and ends out of the horse shed. I'm grateful for that, just glad the place is still standing."

While Elizabeth and Blue Flower prepared a generous meal, Sheriff Barnes and Deck brought them up to date on the events of the last few days.

"I had to go plumb up into the mountains to find Sheriff Barnes," Deck started. "Miss Betsy tole me he was out lookin' fer Injuns."

"Well, I wasn't exactly lookin' for Indians, but I was tryin' to stop some Indian troubles. It seems in the last couple, three months or so that band of Night Wind's had been raidin' around some of the mines. It's rare for an Indian to steal gold, but I've been told several times that Night Wind and his followers were usin' it to buy rifles and whiskey from some gunrunners down on the plains. I kept it as quiet as I could around here and tried to get some help from the Indian agent down in Pagosa.

"That was a bad bunch of cutthroats Night Wind had for friends. But some of them miners is just as bad. I guess they got their fill of their kind gettin' bushwhacked and scalped, and they was thirsty for Indian blood when they got to your place. By then, they was likkered up and it didn't matter what Indian they got their revenge on, but Night Wind's woman would have been hard for them to pass up if they knew who she was. I think it's a good thing you rode out when you did. In fact, I'm surprised that they didn't ride on in and get her that mornin' when you and Deck stopped them. All I can figger is that they hated to risk hurtin' a white woman and figgered they could make you nervous enough to convince you they were going to have her one way or the other.

"I guess when they found you gone the next mornin', they started combing the hills for Indians. About a day or so later, the Indians found them first. Deck had run on to me 'n my boys by then, and we was maybe two or three miles away when we heard the shootin' start. We figgered we'd lay low for a while and let the battle run its course with odds bein' that a good portion of the problem would be taken care of from the sound of all the shootin' we could hear. No use gettin' our heads blown off for a fracas between a bunch of hotheads, them bein' both the miners and the Indians. There wasn't no innocent bystanders involved. Only, this innocent bystander did take a bullet." He nodded toward Deck.

"We rode in carefully after the firing died down, but I guess there was one Indian left with a bullet in the chamber. He had been gut shot and was mad enough to shoot the first white man he could take a bead on. Prob'ly was so crazy with pain, he didn't know who he was shootin' at."

"It was the son of my old friend, Little Wolf," Deck said. "I've 'et at his lodge many a time. I knowed the boy was a little wild. Never figgered he'd shoot me, though. I hope he didn't know it was me." Deck's voice sounded strained, and his head bobbed toward his chest.

"Who won the battle? Were any left alive?" Elizabeth had been turning the bacon automatically while listening with fixed attention.

"Well, I can't say anybody won it," Sheriff Barnes replied. "Nobody knows how many Indians there was for sure, but it seems like two or three might have got away. There was eight dead ones. Five dead miners." He paused to sip his coffee. "But I'd say the people living hereabouts came out the winners. I don't think there will be any more

Indian trouble for a while. I don't think anybody, whites or Indians, will start that stuff agin."

"Was anybody hurt around Elk Fork?" Elizabeth asked.

"Nobody was shot, except for Deck. We knew for several days that Indians were around. There had been a few horses stole. Somebody had broke into Thaddeus Moore's place and got his rifles and then burned the place to the ground. That got people scared enough to make 'em careful. A few families brought their kids to town and left 'em with Widow Simpson and then went back to watch out for their stock and their houses."

Blue Flower had been listening silently; now she spoke. "What about Night Wind's followers and the guns they were buying? I had no idea." She added the last comment almost apologetically.

"Of course you didn't know," Sheriff Barnes replied. "Night Wind was careful and closemouthed except when he got mad. With him gone and most of his bunch dead, there'll be no more trouble."

"But why was Night Wind buying guns? Does anyone know?" Blue Flower's eyebrows were drawn together, changing her usually serene expression.

"Deck has heard rumors that Night Wind planned to take over this part of the mountains. He hated whites and wanted to be rid of them. He felt that Sacred Moon had shown too great a tolerance for white people. Guns would have added a big show of power if there had been any other ideas in the tribe about a successor to Sacred Moon," Sheriff Barnes explained.

Deck spoke up. "I was shore worried about you'ns when I seen that fire. It looked like it was headed in yore direction. I was afraid the smoke might getcha."

"Deck, there wasn't much of a problem. Blue Flower figured out a way to keep the smoke away from us." Elizabeth explained to him how they had protected the entrance to the cave, even including the story about the mountain lion.

Deck was impressed. "I doubt that I could'a done better myself. How come you hung that little cedar bear up out there on the porch post? That thang still gives me the shudders." He could not get it off his mind.

Blue Flower stood up with an air of authority that was totally uncharacteristic of her. She looked at each person very directly, first Deck, then Red Barnes, then Elizabeth. Slowly and with determination, she declared, "We will not talk about it—ever!"

The three quickly turned to a quiet contemplation of their coffee cups.

Their meal was silent until Deck came up with something broachable.

"I'll betcha it's gonna snow perty soon up on them peaks. I got this big toe that starts to hurt ever' fall. I got it stepped on by a horse onct, danged horse purt' near mashed it flat. But onct it starts to painin' me, I start watchin' the high country. An' I always see snow in a couple of weeks or so."

Later Elizabeth asked Blue Flower to go for a pail of water from the stream so that she could talk to Deck and Red Barnes.

"I will talk quickly while Blue Flower is away. That night at the cave, after the mountain lion came, we had another visitor. It was an old Indian dressed in buckskin. I'm not sure, but it seems Blue Flower thought he had something to do with the bear. I fell asleep, and by morning he was gone. Blue Flower would not discuss him with me. She cut me off just as she has done with you today. She did tell me she had given the bear to the old man. And yet when we arrived here, it was hanging just where you saw it today. And Blue Flower declared that it had been blessed!"

Deck appeared to be pondering the whole thing. Sheriff Barnes was tapping his fingers on the table, obviously impatient to get back to town and caring nothing about the tale of the bear or the old man who left it there. He soon stood up and reached for his hat.

"Guess I'll be gettin' back to town. Deck, you stayin' here in case that old Indian comes back lookin' for his bear?"

"I'm stayin', Sheriff Barnes. Somethin' here jest ain't right."

Sheriff Barnes rode off just as Blue Flower arrived with the pail of fresh water.

Deck finished his coffee and then excused himself. "I'll go see to the animals." He turned Pete and Millie loose to graze, then sat down, leaning against the shed and tipping his hat over his eyes as if to doze.

Elizabeth began clearing the table of food and dishes. "Blue Flower, you should rest." She urged the Indian woman into the bedroom.

Finally alone, Elizabeth cleaned the kitchen, glad to have something to keep her hands busy while her mind worked. In a few minutes, she peeked into the bedroom. Blue Flower was breathing evenly and deeply, obviously asleep. Elizabeth quickly stepped outside. Approaching Deck, she spoke softly, "Deck, are you sleeping?"

"No, ma'am, I'm settin' here, thinkin'."

She sat down on the grass near him. "What did you mean when you told Sheriff Barnes that something was not right here?"

"I can't put my finger on jest what's wrong. I jest know I've got a prickly feelin'."

"A prickly feeling? What do you mean?"

"Yeah, kind of spooky like. It's got somethin' to do with that bear thang."

"It's just an Indian relic, Deck," she said, denying to herself that the amulet made her feel a little spooky, too. "After Blue Flower gave the amulet to the old man, he must have decided to return it. She must have told him who we were, and he knew we would be coming back here.

I couldn't understand what they were saying, but I know she and Hooded Hawk talked long into the night."

Deck jerked his head toward her so quickly that he almost threw off his hat. His face held an expression of disbelief.

"Who did you say?"

"I said Blue Flower and Hooded Hawk talked long into the night."

Deck's expression turned to one of fear. "Miss Elizabeth, are you sure? It can't be!" He was almost stuttering. "Hooded Hawk died years before my time!"

"Deck, calm down. I'm sure this is just someone with the same name."

"No, ma'am! Injuns don't use the name of the dead agin. Lots of 'em won't even speak the name of the dead. Did Blue Flower tell you his name?"

"Well, she did say, just once, that his name was Hooded Hawk. I had pressed her, but she seemed reluctant to tell me. She has refused to talk about it anymore. Who was this Hooded Hawk supposed to have been?"

"I don't want to talk about it either, Miss Elizabeth. Let's get that Indian woman and that danged bear away from here." Deck's face held a wild expression.

"Deck, let's think this thing out. I'm sure Blue Flower wants to get back to her children now that things seem to be safe. But if she wants to stay here a little longer to see if Thornton McRae shows up, she's welcome. I don't like that danged bear, as you call it, hanging over my door. But it is part of their beliefs, not ours. It has no power to bring luck, good or bad, to any people except the tribe to whom it belongs." Elizabeth knew she was grabbing blindly for something that might bring Deck back to his senses. He seemed to be calming down, so she continued, hoping Blue Flower would take a long nap. Soon she had him answering her questions and gradually brought him around to telling her the story of Hooded Hawk.

Hooded Hawk was the brother of Crested Owl, a most powerful and respected chief. Hooded Hawk had been indiscreet with Crested Owl's wife. When Crested Owl found them together, Crested Owl had experienced a fit of passion and had slain his brother, driving a knife through his heart. Then in penance, Crested Owl left the tribe for a period of fasting and purification.

"Miss Elizabeth, nobody ever knowed what happened to Chief Crested Owl. By the time they come to know he wasn't coming back there wasn't no way for any of 'em to figger out what happened to him."

Elizabeth surmised what had happened to Crested Owl. He must have been the fatally injured Indian her mother had written about so many years ago.

Suddenly, Elizabeth heard a piercing cry from the cabin. She gathered her skirts around her and ran toward the door.

When Elizabeth rushed in, Blue Flower was sitting on the edge of the bed, panting slightly. "Elizabeth, I must get back to my children."

"You've had a bad dream, haven't you?"

Blue Flower nodded and repeated, "I must get back to my children."

"But how? You are still weak."

"Maybe Deck will take me. I know I cannot walk that far yet. But I must get back."

"Please wait at least a few days. You have not eaten well since your illness. A few good meals will make you much stronger."

Blue Flower repeated, "I must go."

"Let's wait and talk about it tomorrow."

Blue Flower agreed to that comment, but she immediately arose and went into the forest. Elizabeth followed her, not hiding, but trying to remain inconspicuous. Blue Flower went to a large cedar tree and began breaking off the dead, low hanging branches. She gathered several of them in her arms and returned to the cabin, where she placed them in a mound below the post where the bear hung.

Finally, Elizabeth could not contain her questions, "Why are you doing that?"

Blue Flower responded without emotion, "It will keep away unwanted spirits. Indian spirits will not be here."

Elizabeth was sick of the talk of spirits, and for a brief moment, she was sick of one particular Indian.

CHAPTER 19

WHEN THE SO-CALLED Hooded Hawk left the cave that dark and smoky night, his heart was filled with triumph. The amulet he carried on the thong around his neck gave him an unforeseen advantage. His sole purpose for the visit to Blue Flower had been to awe her with a visit from an ancestor long gone; to frighten her with this visit into complying with his wishes. Now he knew it was quite possible that around his neck hung the key to making the Ute woman his vassal through her fear and veneration of the amulet. He knew the woman with her was Thornton McRae's white woman, and he knew where they would be returning.

Hooded Hawk pulled a white man's bandanna from his stolen Ute buckskins and tied it over his face to close out the smoke and ash as he crept through the dry streambed.

The aging Indian made his way slowly toward the east, away from the flames and the smoke of the fire, toward the camp of his Arapaho brothers. Raging Wolf had been carefully chosen for this impersonation because of his appearance. Born many years ago of an Arapaho warrior and a captive Ute woman, he had inherited more of his mother's physical characteristics than his father's. Raging Wolf had heard the story of the tragedy between Crested Owl and his brother, Hooded Hawk, since he had been a child, although it had always been told secretively, partly out of reverence for the dead and partly in deference to the power Crested Owl had once held among the Indians of the mountains.

The spirits must be with us, he thought. He had never given his name to Blue Flower until he learned that she had an amulet that she thought belonged to Crested Owl many years ago. Then he could not resist using the well-known story.

Raging Wolf assumed the carving was traded to the white woman by some Mexican who had made it himself and used the well-known story to go along with it. As he crept through the dry streambed, Raging Wolf was smirking at the awe and respect Blue Flower had shown him. He could tell she was totally convinced that he was the spirit of Hooded Hawk. It had been difficult for him to suppress a whoop when she had gone into the dark corner of the cave, brought forth the amulet, and placed it reverently into his hands. She had told him of its origins and how it had come to be in her hands. She told him of the recent misfortunes that had befallen her since the amulet had come into her possession.

Those misfortunes he had witnessed day-by-day as he had observed her almost continuously. Many times, it had been tempting to snatch the wounded woman, but each time caution had held him back because of the nearby presence of Indians and white men searching for each other. He had known her physical condition would have made escape difficult if he had been seen with her and would probably jeopardize his goals.

It had long been known by the Arapaho that Night Wind had ambitions to become chief of the mountain Ute people at Sacred Moon's death, extending his influence to a much greater degree through the tribe. They feared Night Wind because of his vicious night raids against their homes on the nearby plains, and they loathed him for his frequent cruelty to the Arapaho women and children. In spite of the Arapaho attempts to watch his movements closely, he was elusive. Their surveillance told them that Night Wind was obtaining arms from the white gunrunners of the plains. But their best efforts could not lead them to the cache of weapons. Somehow, the small band of night-riding Utes always slipped away from them on the dark, remote mountain trails. They knew if Night Wind acquired a significant store of weapons and eventually became chief, the Arapaho would surely be driven from their tribal range or slaughtered.

The Arapaho could not be sure that Blue Flower knew where the cache of weapons was. It was quite plausible that she would know, since she was a well-respected woman of the Ute and since Night Wind was known to be excessively talkative when he had been drinking the white man's whiskey. However, if the Arapaho could not find out from her where the weapons were, they were quite sure they could convince Sacred Moon to purchase her safety with many horses and perhaps a few guns.

When Raging Wolf finally reached his camp, his Arapaho brothers accepted his news with great pleasure as he told them about his meeting with Blue Flower and dangled the amulet in front of the low fire.

CHAPTER 20

THE NIGHT HAD been a cold one, and morning showed a light frost on the grasses in the clearing around the cabin. Elizabeth had breakfast almost ready when Deck came in, greeting them with the comment, "Snow's not far off, I reckon."

Blue Flower jerked her head up from where she was stirring the fire. Elizabeth could see the urgency in her eyes.

"Perhaps you are right, Blue Flower, about getting back to your children before winter sets in. Maybe Deck could see about borrowing a horse for you from someone in town or maybe renting one at the stable. I'm sure Deck could see you to your people. I'll pay for the rental of the horse if Deck will see that it gets back safely."

Deck jumped at the chance, eager to get the Indian woman on her way. "I'll take care of it, Miss Elizabeth. But climbin' over all them rocks, Millie has throwed a shoe. I don't want to leave you 'n her here without gittin' it fixed. If it's all right with you, I'll take her into town 'n git it took care of, 'n I can git a horse lined up for Blue Flower."

"I would appreciate it, Deck. I'll give you the money after we eat. Sit down, breakfast is ready."

Deck rode off on Millie as soon as the meal was finished, and Elizabeth set about clearing the table.

Blue Flower fell into silence; Elizabeth did not attempt conversation, but left her alone with her thoughts. Soon Blue Flower said, "I want to be outdoors. I think I will go for a walk."

Elizabeth understood her need to be alone after the two

of them had been together almost constantly for several days.

"There are some wild plums to the west of here, just south of the stream. With the drought, they have been late ripening this year. If you want, you could take a bucket and bring some back if the frost hasn't got them yet."

This seemed to please Blue Flower. "Yes, I will bring back some plums if they are still good." She took the bucket Elizabeth offered and left.

Elizabeth also welcomed the solitude and the feeling of security that had been lacking for so many days. She remembered a piece of embroidery that she had not worked on for some time. As soon as the kitchen was cleaned, she pulled out the tablecloth with its half-finished pattern of daisies and sat on the front step in the sun, handling her needle quickly and expertly while her mind roamed.

The sun was high before Elizabeth began to wonder why Blue Flower's walk was keeping her away so long. She knew it was not more than a mile to the plum bushes. Still she continued with her embroidery, knowing that Blue Flower had probably felt as oppressed as she by their enforced togetherness.

It was only when her stomach began to growl for lunch that Elizabeth became concerned enough to put her stitchery aside. She wondered if Blue Flower could have fallen, perhaps misjudging her strength and the distance she could walk so soon after her illness. Closing the door to the cabin, she began to walk hurriedly in the direction Blue Flower had taken.

In a matter of twenty minutes or so, Elizabeth saw the plum bushes in a sunny area on the eastern side of a low rise. Pausing, she looked around and called Blue Flower's name. Hearing no answer, she continued to walk. As she neared the bushes, Elizabeth saw the bucket. It was lying on its side, underneath one of the larger bushes, with plump fruit spilling onto the ground. Elizabeth grew alarmed; she looked around cautiously, peering into the bushes, hoping to see some sign of Blue Flower, but fearing she would see Indians peering back at her. Her heart was thudding with a fear she could not suppress. She could not bring herself to call out again, but turned and began to run for home as fast as she could, feeling inexplicably frightened.

Breathlessly, Elizabeth snatched Pete's bridle from the wall of the storage shed as she passed by. Darting into the cabin, she grabbed a kitchen knife, returned to the porch, and slashed the thong holding the now-detested amulet to the post. She ran in and tossed it into the fireplace. With difficulty, she got the bridle on Pete and led him to a rock from which she could mount the mule. Kicking her heels into his sides, she got the animal going at a surprisingly fast, if uneven, lope. She found that by kicking him firmly and yelling, she could keep the animal moving at a good pace while she fought to stay seated. They were almost a mile from the cabin before she realized she had left the rifle standing in a corner near the door.

She rode into town and headed up the street for the sheriff's office. She didn't even realize she was passing the blacksmith shop until she saw Deck run out declaring, "Why, that's ol' Pete and Miss Elizabeth!"

By now Pete had lost the head of steam and was ambling along at his usual pace. When Deck approached them, Elizabeth realized how unseemly it must look for a lady to be sitting bareback astride a mule. She slipped her left leg over Pete's rump and landed with a soft thud in the dusty street.

Elizabeth's words came tumbling out as she grabbed Deck's uninjured arm and half dragged him up the street toward the sheriff's office.

"Miss Elizabeth, she prob'ly just got lost in the woods," Deck protested.

But Elizabeth would not listen to him or to Sheriff

Barnes after she had repeated her story to him. Nothing would calm her until Red Barnes agreed to take a few men to search for Blue Flower and the kidnappers who Elizabeth feared were responsible for the woman's disappearance.

The sheriff suggested Elizabeth stay with his family until he and Deck returned to town.

When the party of four arrived at the place where Elizabeth had found the spilled bucket of plums, they had to agree that the woman might be right. Jim Bodie, an excellent tracker, found two sets of moccasin prints, small ones made by Blue Flower, and a larger set made by a man. There was no sign of a struggle, so he could not be sure if Blue Flower had been abducted or if she went willingly with someone she knew. Sheriff Barnes knew he must assume the worst and follow up on it. He was not going to return to town without news for Elizabeth.

"It's that danged bear thang agin', Sheriff. It's been mighty strange around here ever since it turned up," Deck declared.

Sheriff Barnes could only partially agree. "Well, things *have* been busy hereabouts lately."

CHAPTER 21

THE AUTUMN SUN had been warm that morning, lifting Blue Flower's spirits as she filled the bucket with the wild fruit. The bucket was almost full when she either heard or felt the presence of someone else; she was not sure what had alarmed her. Turning quickly, she dropped the bucket with a cry as she looked into the eyes of Hooded Hawk, who stood little more than an arm's length away.

Raging Wolf saw the fear in her eyes and was pleased. "You must come with me." He spoke sternly.

Blue Flower stepped backward, stumbling into the bushes. "No! No! I must not!"

The man realized she had misunderstood him. He spoke a little more gently. "I do not mean into the spirit world. You must come with me. I need your help. You must help your people."

"Help my people?" Fear and confusion showed in her voice.

"Do not be afraid. Come with me," he repeated. "We must talk. I need your help." He turned and walked away as if he knew she would follow.

Her heart pounding, Blue Flower slowly forced herself to put one foot in front of the other. She was afraid not to obey the spirit.

They had not walked far when they came upon two ponies that Raging Wolf had tied nearby. Silently, he mounted one and motioned for her to mount the other. She was glad to do so, because fear had made her legs weak and wobbly.

Blue Flower had lost track of time and the distance they

had traveled when they suddenly emerged into a small clearing. Raging Wolf had chosen it carefully for their meeting. It was very secluded, being surrounded by a thick forest of oak and impossible to be seen from more than a few feet away. More importantly, there was an eerie air about the place, lent by an ancient burned-out stump of a magnificent tree, now a blackened finger arising some ten or twelve feet from the forest floor. Its age was obvious: enough time had passed for the surrounding trees to have grown to soaring heights since the fire that had left this ancient one a charred ruin.

Raging Wolf dismounted and seated himself with his back to the stump. He motioned for Blue Flower to sit facing him. "It is here we will talk."

He began by talking in rambling terms about the purification of the tribe. Blue Flower became more confused and frightened than ever when he spoke of purging the tribe of all things pertaining to the white man. She thought of her half-white son, and terror filled her heart. Was he suggesting expelling her son from the tribe? The question burst from her lips.

Seeing another tool that he could use to extract cooperation from the young woman, Raging Wolf pondered for a moment.

"That may not be necessary if we can achieve sufficient cleansing in other ways." He paused a few moments to let the importance of his comment penetrate.

"What do you mean?" Her voice was little more than a whisper.

"Blue Flower," he called her by name for the first time. "We must rid our tribe of the curse of the white man's weapons. You must help me do this." He spoke more urgently than he had previously.

Blue Flower thought of the few guns that she knew were within her village and felt that the request was a strange one. "I will do what I can. How can I help? I have no such weapon."

"But you know where there are many. You must tell me where they are. They must be destroyed."

The woman's eyes had stared at the ground during the entire discourse.

"Look at me, Blue Flower!" he commanded.

She did so, trying to avoid seeing the blazing hatred in his dark eyes.

"Where are the many guns Night Wind got from our enemies, the white man?"

Surprise showed clearly in her eyes. "Guns from white men?" she echoed. "I do not know of such. What do you mean?"

Raging Wolf thought he should believe her from the expression on her face and the questions in her voice, but he continued to query and to threaten her with subtle references to her son until he was satisfied from the desperate, fearful look on her face that she knew nothing.

It was then that he raised his right hand with a gesture that brought four warriors from the surrounding brush.

Blue Flower wanted to scream with anger, but she choked off any sound. She took in the garments they wore, the style of their hair, the weapons they carried, and she knew they were Arapaho, the biggest enemy of the Ute, even more so than the white men who had invaded their mountains. She looked at her captor and knew this was no ancestral spirit sent to cleanse her people. This was an Arapaho hoping to use her to obtain weapons. And she had just declared her ignorance of the one thing that made her valuable to them.

"You will kill me now," she stated simply, hoping that was the worst they had in mind for her.

"Not yet. Perhaps Sacred Moon will think your life is worth a few guns or a few horses. We shall see," Raging Wolf said chillingly.

With that, he commanded her to mount the horse. He tied her hands to the saddle, and the six of them rode off at a rapid trot.

On the long ride to the north, Blue Flower tried to sort out her thoughts. All this talk of guns and white men! She began to realize what Night Wind's hunting trips had meant. It was true that he had brought back a few deer, elk, or antelope, but in retrospect how dismally small the amount of game had been.

The late afternoon wind began to grow sharp, and Blue Flower wished momentarily for the coat that McRae had given her. But when she thought about the trouble it seemed to have brought, she decided it was better to be cold.

As the sun dropped below the mountains on her left, Blue Flower dreaded the stop for the night. It was not yet dark when they approached a campsite that looked as if it had been occupied for some time. Bones from past meals were scattered around; ashes had built up at the cooking fires; and the three tepees showed signs of slackness, indicating that no women occupied the camp to set them up in the precise manner all women were taught. The men released her from the ropes binding her to the saddle and shoved her roughly into one of the tepees.

An hour or so later, Raging Wolf flung back the door flap and indicated that she should come outside. Fearfully, she did so, wondering what awaited her at the hands of the five Arapaho.

Raging Wolf gave her a bowl and pointed toward the pot on the fire. Blue Flower dipped her bowl into the stew that bubbled inside and waited for her portion to cool. When it had done so, she fished out the meat with her fingers and drank the broth. After finishing her meal, Blue Flower sat silently with her head down, wishing that one of the men would tell her to return to her tepee. However, Raging

Wolf soon placed a rifle on the ground in front of her. She was certain it was Thornton McRae's rifle.

Her throat constricted so that she could hardly draw a breath, but she made no sign of her emotion. Since Raging Wolf had Thornton McRae's rifle, they must have killed him. She also realized the Arapaho were trying to frighten her with this subtle threat; even though their technique was working, she refused to give any sign. She sat motionless until Raging Wolf indicated that she could leave the fire. She rose with grace and disappeared into the tepee.

The night was a long and sleepless one for Blue Flower. It was cold, but she had a sleeping robe for warmth. Her belly was full, and she could not complain that she had been mistreated. Yet her heart ached—with thoughts of her children, whom she might never again see, with thoughts of Thornton McRae, who was likely dead. Would Sacred Moon give guns or horses for her life? Would Thornton McRae's white wife be glad she was gone and forget that she had ever existed? She lay miserably in the darkness, almost afraid to move for fear of reminding the Arapaho of her presence.

The night brought the first snowfall of the season. When dawn approached, Blue Flower breathed with relief that she had passed the night unharmed. Crawling over to the door flap with the buffalo robe still wrapped around her, she peeked out into the gray dawn, made grayer still by the heavy clouds that shrouded the pines and by the thin blanket of white that lay on the ground. A sprinkling of snow was still falling. She wrapped the robe more tightly around her body, hoping that the Arapaho would be inclined to let the day drift by without much activity.

It was probably an hour later when Raging Wolf jerked the door flap open and declared, "Food is ready."

Blue Flower gave him a glowering look and pulled the buffalo robe over her head. She had no desire for food or for the companionship of those whose fire she was being forced to share. She remained in the tepee through the day, peering out from time to time to spy on her captors. Each time, there were no more than three to be seen. She assumed that the Arapaho who were not present had been sent with a message for Sacred Moon.

It was thirst that finally drove her from seclusion. The night was dark and still when Blue Flower drew aside the door flap and reached outside to scoop up some of the snow in her palm. She looked across at the guard who was sitting beneath a tree across the darkened clearing. Seeing no movement on his part, she hastily stuffed her mouth with snow. Then her hand froze in midair. She stared into the face of a white man who had just appeared from the side of her shelter.

He was crouching low and motioned for her to come. She slid from the tepee as silently as possible, hardly wondering who her rescuer was. When the two of them reached the shelter of the trees, they both glanced back to see if their activity had been detected. The camp remained dark and silent. The guard still leaned against the tree, and Blue Flower knew he must be dead because the white man ignored the guard's presence, not even glancing in his direction. Silently, they crept through the darkness and were soon joined by three more white men. She first saw the big, hulking figure of Sheriff Barnes to her right; just beyond him was Deck's slender form. To the left of her rescuer was another white man whom she did not know. She could tell all four of the men were wise to the ways of the woods because hardly a sound could be heard. They came upon their horses and, moving as silently as possible, untied them and led them away.

When they had put sufficient distance between themselves and the Indian camp, they mounted their horses. Pulling Blue Flower up behind him, Sheriff Barnes asked, "Are you all right?"

"Yes," she replied. A question still bothered her. "Are you just going to let those Arapaho get away?"

"I try not to mess in Indian business. Since they didn't harm you, I figger it's best to let the Indians handle their trouble by themselves." He motioned to the man who had come into the camp for her. "This here's Jim Bodie, and the other fellow there is Henry Jenkins."

Blue Flower thanked them warmly. As the five of them rode away at a quiet pace, Blue Flower wondered if Sheriff Barnes knew his man had killed the Arapaho guard.

Sheriff Barnes was filled with questions for Blue Flower, but he forced himself to keep quiet on the way back to Elk Fork.

CHAPTER 22

ELIZABETH WAS MISERABLE at Betsy's. The children annoyed her, and she was concerned about Blue Flower and the men who were searching for her. But most of all she was angry with Thornton McRae for putting her through the things she had experienced. She wasn't really sure why she blamed Trap for everything; she thought it was similar to Deck's blaming the bear amulet for all their misfortunes. Even the playful kittens didn't lift her mood.

Betsy could sense Elizabeth's restlessness. It was she who finally suggested that they visit Mona. They rode to Mona's, but Elizabeth returned from the brief visit as depressed as before.

She kept remembering Deck's words, "Let's get rid of that danged bear and the Indian woman." She felt guilt for agreeing with him. Yet she wanted to be rid of Thornton McRae and his Indian woman. She wanted to go back to the cabin, the only home of her own she had known since her parents died. She wanted to resume her routine life—with no Indians, miners, or bears to mar the days. Still, her sense of relief was acute when she saw the men riding up the road with Blue Flower.

The entire party crowded into Betsy's small living room as Betsy bustled about the kitchen, warming food and making coffee for everyone. Red Barnes brought Blue Flower a glass of water, then seated himself beside her.

"Blue Flower, I ain't sure yet why them Arapaho took you. In fact, until we found that Arapaho camp and watched it for a while, we wasn't even sure if you had been taken or if you had left with people you knew. Tell us what happened."

Blue Flower told them about Night Wind and the guns, and the plans that the Arapaho had for her. She seemed embarrassed to explain how she had been fooled into thinking that she had encountered the spirit form of Hooded Hawk.

As soon as Elizabeth had heard most of the explanation, she quietly left the room and walked down to Ben's Emporium.

"Miz McRae, so glad to see you. It's good to hear that Blue Flower is safely back. What can I help you with today?" Ben Barnes was ebullient, as he usually was when Elizabeth McRae came around. He openly admired the woman and secretly envied Trap McRae.

"Mr. Barnes, those rooms you built upstairs, I'd like to rent one for a night or two."

"Why, yes, ma'am, of course. But ain't you comfortable over at Betsy's?" He took a swipe with a dusting towel at the orange cat perched on a bolt of calico lying on the counter.

Elizabeth felt her throat constrict as it always did when she was close to tears. She tried to maintain her composure.

"Mr. Barnes, it's not that at all. It's just that . . ." she paused a moment, unsure whether to tell the truth or not. "It's just that, well, frankly, I'm sick to death of Blue Flower. She has brought all this trouble to me. I want to go home, but I'm afraid to as long as she's around. Who knows what will happen next? Deck was right days ago when he told me I should ask her to leave."

Ben didn't know what to say to a woman who was saddled with her husband's Indian wife, although he felt sympathy with Elizabeth's plight. He knew she had been uncommonly generous toward the Indian woman, so he offered his own generosity.

"You move right in, Miz McRae. I won't even charge you.

Don't seem like there's gonna be a run on my rooms for a while anyways."

That afternoon, Elizabeth asked Deck to ride with her to the cabin to bring fresh clothing into town for herself and Blue Flower. On the way, she asked, "Deck, winter is coming soon. Would you stay with me at the cabin for a while?"

Deck thought long and hard, spitting a stream of tobacco juice to the right of Pete's ears while his mind was working. "No, ma'am, I guess I wouldn't just now. That Indian woman's brung so much trouble, I think you and me would do good to stay clear of her."

"Deck, I didn't mean to bring Blue Flower back out here."

"Well, give it a few days, Miss Elizabeth. I think the problem will maybe see itself through. I heard Blue Flower tell Sheriff Barnes that if he didn't loan her a horse to ride back to Sacred Moon's camp, that she'd steal one and go anyway. Maybe we can get back to yore place after ever'body in the country has a chance to know that the Indian woman's gone. She's sure been a pack of trouble. You did tell me that you got rid of that danged bear thang, didn't ya?"

"The bear is gone, Deck." She didn't tell him that she had merely flung it into the fireplace. "Blue Flower didn't mean to cause all this trouble; she's had some misfortune is all."

"Yes, ma'am, if that's what you say. But I don't know why her misfortune has to involve all of us. We should've left her in the woods that day we found her. Of course, you did get yer coat back."

"I'm sure you don't mean that, Deck. You're just fed up with all the problems, and I admit that I am too." Elizabeth didn't mention that the coat was so fouled with bloodstains that it was doubtful that it could ever be worn.

When they arrived at the cabin, Deck waited outside for her to pack a few items of clothing.

Elizabeth was tempted to stay and send a few things back to town for Blue Flower, but she knew it would be unwise. So, she carefully retrieved the cedar bear from the fireplace, wrapped it carefully, and began to pack a few skirts, blouses, and underwear, resolving to see that Sheriff Barnes cooperated with Blue Flower's demand for a horse.

Elizabeth and Deck rode back into town late in the afternoon. As they passed the blacksmith shop and livery stable on the west end of the street, they could see a crowd gathering at the other end, where the sheriff's office stood. Elizabeth urged Millie on, wanting to hurry along and see what was happening.

The first person on the outskirts of the crowd whom Elizabeth had a chance to speak to was Widow Simpson.

"Mrs. Simpson, what's going on?"

"It's that Thornton McRae!" Widow Simpson was so distracted, trying to peer through the crowd to see what was taking place, that she did not realize that she was talking to Mrs. McRae. "That man, they call him Deacon something or other, Deacon Romine, I believe, brought him in just about blown apart. Some accident having to do with guns and dynamite." Widow Simpson scurried off to another part of the crowd where she would have a better view of the goings-on as Mrs. Tupelo arrived with her medicine bag and rushed to the wounded man's side.

Elizabeth looked beyond the crowd and saw Blue Flower running as fast as she could down the road toward the wagon where Thornton McRae lay. Elizabeth turned Millie and rode back to Barnes Emporium, where she and Deck unloaded the clothing and personal articles she had packed. Without speaking, she went into her room and closed the door.

A few hours later, dusk was gathering and Elizabeth's small room grew dark; she sat in the gloom with her thoughts and feelings crowding in. Suddenly she thought she heard a scratching noise. She cleared her head and listened; there it was again. A scratching noise came from the door, and then a whisper, "Miss Elizabeth." She recognized Deck's voice.

"Deck, come in," she said as she opened the door.

Deck looked troubled as he rushed in as if someone was pursuing him.

"What's wrong, Deck?"

"Ma'am, I don't think you are gonna take kindly to what I'm about to say."

"Just go ahead and say it, Deck." She poured him a glass of water from the pitcher that Ben Barnes had left on the tiny night table beside the bed.

He gulped quickly before he spoke. "I've been out in the woods just for a little walk. But there's an Injun man that wants to talk to you. I've done tole Sheriff Barnes about 'im. He says it's safe if you want to go talk to 'im."

"Slow down a little, Deck. I don't know what you are talking about. Let's start from the beginning. There is an Indian who wants to talk to me?" She tried to speak slowly to let Deck's agitation settle.

"Yes, ma'am."

"Do you know who it is?" In the back of her mind she feared it was the old one to whom Blue Flower had given the bear.

"It's Sacred Moon. The one Blue Flower told us about!"

"Her father-in-law? Why does he want to speak to me?"

"I told him about how you cared for Blue Flower, you 'n me, whilst she was sick. I guess he wants to thank you."

"Is he alone?"

"Yes, ma'am . . . well, not exactly. He's got some warriors with 'im, but he knowed you'd be scared of 'em. He said he would meet you by hisself. He tole me where he would be."

"You said Sheriff Barnes said it would be safe for me to talk to him."

"He shore did."

"And what do you think?"

"I've always heered that Sacred Moon is a man of his word. If he asks a lady to meet with him, she'd be safer'n if she was home in bed."

Elizabeth thought about it for a moment while leaning against the door. Why she would consider meeting with the old man puzzled her for a few seconds, but then curiosity got the better hand.

"Will you go with me?"

"Wouldn't want you to go without me, ma'am."

"Then let's go. But first wait for me just outside the door for a moment. Let me freshen my hair."

As soon as Deck was on the other side of the closed door, she reached into the stack of clothing she had brought for Blue Flower and retrieved the cedar bear. Tucking it into her skirt pocket, she took a glance at herself in the mirror above the nightstand, smoothed a hair or two, and joined Deck.

He led her on foot outside of town, where they came upon Millie and Pete, saddled and tied in a small oak grove. Elizabeth looked at Deck in surprise.

"Why is Millie here? You were sure I would agree to meet Sacred Moon?"

Deck looked at the ground and kicked a stone with his toe. "Miss Elizabeth, you got the spirit of a bear. I knowed you'd come."

For a moment she was shaken by Deck's comment about the amulet. Then it occurred to her he meant something else by *the spirit of a bear*. Elizabeth mounted the horse and followed Deck in a circuitous route through the forest.

They came upon Sacred Moon sitting before a low fire in a small clearing. Deck, of course, knew where the old man would be, but his unexpected appearance startled Elizabeth.

She sat on her horse for a few moments, unsure what to do.

"You may dismount in safety. Have no fear," Sacred Moon said. He rose as she got off the horse.

"I have even prepared some of the white man's favorite drink—coffee."

Elizabeth was immediately impressed by his graciousness. As she and Deck dismounted, Sacred Moon motioned for them to sit by the fire, indicating a sleek, smooth deerskin across from the buffalo robe on which he had been seated. She and Deck seated themselves as Sacred Moon poured coffee from a blackened iron coffeepot into sturdy cups of pottery. The dichotomy of the white man's cast iron and the native pottery was not lost on Elizabeth.

"I thank you for coming. I am indebted to you for what you have done to help Blue Flower. Deck has explained your efforts to me. They have been immense."

Elizabeth felt in awe of Sacred Moon. He was a man with obvious strength and character. She gathered her thoughts about her for a reply, never feeling rushed to respond.

"I have been fortunate in being able to assist Blue Flower," she replied simply. "She is an honorable woman."

"Blue Flower means a great deal to me. She was the wife of my son." He carefully omitted the name, Elizabeth noticed. "She is the mother of my grandson. I, too, feel she is a woman to be honored. The other boy, the son of your man, McRae, is considered by our people to be my grandson, as I consider him such."

"Please, sir, McRae is not my man. I was married to him in a legal ceremony, but he and I have never been husband and wife. We never will be." She felt her voice growing loud and repressed further comments and her emotions.

She changed the subject and tried to speak in a more controlled manner. "If you will, Sacred Moon, tell us how you came to be here just as Thornton McRae was brought in. It is not a coincidence, I'm sure."

CHAPTER 23

WHEN MORNING HAD arisen over the Ute encampment, Blue Flower and Night Wind had not returned. Sacred Moon rose early and knew that things had gone awry. He had heard the slight noises in the night that told him his son's followers were leaving the village. He hurried to the lodge next to his, knowing that Big Thunder would help him sort out his thoughts and decide on a course of action.

Sacred Moon, Big Thunder, and three braves rode out before the sun was high in the sky. Before midday, they had found the body of Sacred Moon's son. Night Wind was lying in a small grove of young trees, his head toward the east, with a blanket spread over him and fastened at the corners with heavy rocks.

Sacred Moon dispatched one of the braves to return to his village with news of the death and instructions to recover the body. His only comment on the death of his son was "It was an honorable fight. Great pains were taken to protect the body so that it would not be desecrated."

Then, with an anguished expression on his face he added, "We must find McRae."

Sacred Moon knew that there were answers to be obtained about his son's activities and his death that only McRae could explain. He grieved deeply inside for the loss of his son, but at the same time, he was profoundly grateful that he need worry no more about Night Wind's eventual leadership of his people. The people and their future were much more important than a father's grief for the death of his son.

It took them no more than a day to find McRae. He was

holed up deep in a canyon where Night Wind's men had
him trapped. He was not wounded, but there were bodies
of three young Indians at the mouth of the canyon, men
whom Sacred Moon recognized as followers of Night
Wind.

Thornton McRae had heard the horses coming, but they
did not seem to be riding with aggression in mind. He sat
and watched. When he saw Sacred Moon, he did not know
whether to be relieved that it was an old friend or frightened because he had killed the man's son.

"Sacred Moon, is that you?" he shouted.

The Indians drew up their horses just across a little
chasm from where McRae watched.

"It is, McRae. You killed my son."

"I did." McRae replied. "I had no choice," he shouted
across to where they sat beneath two large oaks.

"Where is Blue Flower? Is she with you?"

"I don't know where Blue Flower is. We got separated
along the trail. We need to talk, Sacred Moon. Come in
alone."

Sacred Moon rode in by himself. "McRae, you killed my
son. Why?"

"You had no idea that Night Wind was gathering arms?"
he questioned.

"Gathering arms from what source?"

"Your son had been buying arms—guns, ammunition,
possibly a cannon—from the runners on the plains."

"How can you prove this to me?" Sacred Moon doubted
that McRae would make such an accusation if he were not
positive of its truth. Nor did he doubt that it was within his
son's nature to do such a thing. But he did wonder how
the white man could know.

"I, too, buy ammunition from the gunrunners. I hear
talk, and I talk to those around me. I think you have hidden your head if you do not know what your son has been

doing. Night Wind was a murderer. I just killed him first, before he got me and Blue Flower."

Suddenly, out of the trees appeared Big Thunder and the braves. Sacred Moon promptly ended the conversation.

"We will talk alone later, in the morning perhaps." He turned away, then turned back with a rare expression of sadness on his face. "Perhaps you are right about my son. I am not yet sure."

McRae knew he would not be there in the morning. It was past midnight, he judged, by the time he felt confident that the sleep of the Utes was sound enough to allow him to go undetected. He slipped through the trees like a cloud, trailing his horse behind him, smirking a little to himself that it had been so easy to leave the Indians behind. Of course, he knew that Sacred Moon would be in pursuit.

McRae had a pretty good idea where the guns were stashed. He had not roamed the mountains blindly over the last several years. His leg troubled him, but he put the pain out of his mind. Since Night Wind's followers had pursued him, he was confident Blue Flower had made it safely to Elk Fork. He was intent on one thing, and that was getting to the guns before Sacred Moon could do so.

He made his plans carefully as he traveled, knowing that he could do nothing about the guns without dynamite. His dynamite was far behind, down some lonesome trail where his packhorse had wandered. He headed for the Lucky Lady, the closest hard-rock mine in his vicinity.

Stealing the dynamite was easy. From there, he climbed still higher, planning what he would do once he found the stash of weapons.

Sacred Moon was growing old, and McRae could not guess what young buck might follow him. If a new leader used the guns to wage war it could lead to total annihilation of the Ute nation. McRae lost all thought of himself in his desire to destroy the guns.

As he left the mine, he did not realize that he was being followed by Deacon Romine from the Lucky Lady. The man had set out on his trail shortly after Trap had taken the explosives. McRae kept close watch because he figured that Sacred Moon was somewhere not too far behind. He knew it would be useless to try to conceal his trail, so he didn't waste the time except to slow them down by such tactics as wading his horse through water or riding across rock whenever possible.

He pushed his horse farther and farther up into the mountains where the air became thin and cold. For some time, McRae had known that Night Wind was moving weapons. There was nothing unusual or menacing about a brave buying a few guns. It was only after it was clear that Night Wind was stockpiling an arsenal that McRae understood the dire consequences for the Utes.

With Night Wind dead, this stash of weapons, left in the wrong hands, could lead to murder and desecration throughout the mountains and the surrounding plains.

He searched several caves and abandoned mine shafts before finding where the weapons were hidden. Row after row of cartons of guns and ammunition were there. He had only to wire the explosives.

He was relieved that the pursuing Indians had not caught up with him and there had been no confrontation over the weapons.

He began wiring, stringing firing cap to detonator. He was just outside the mine shaft when a bullet screamed past him and buried itself in the stack of dynamite just inside the tunnel. The explosion was magnificent in its power. McRae felt the strength of it through his entire body and could only exult in the fact that it had not killed him instantly as he felt the blood oozing from his wounds while he fought his way back into painful reality.

When he awakened he saw Sacred Moon, Big Thunder, and the other Ute warriors gathered around him, shaking the scalp of an Arapaho over him in triumph. It was only then that he knew the Arapaho as well as Sacred Moon had been on his backtrail.

"We are grateful that the white man, Deacon Romine, helped us bring him in. We did not know what sort of welcome the Ute would receive," Sacred Moon added when the account was finished.

Sacred Moon's eyebrows puckered in thought. "McRae destroyed the guns. Perhaps it is best. The Ute could have used them, but they could have been used against us as well."

Elizabeth stood up and pulled the cedar bear amulet from her pocket.

"I'd like to give this to you. It should have been in your family for all this time instead of in mine. Blue Flower can tell you how I came to be in possession of it. I will go now." At the edge of the clearing, she turned back. "Thank you, Sacred Moon, for having me here and offering your appreciation and your explanation."

Elizabeth did not talk on their way back to town. Deck was disappointed that she would not discuss their meeting with Sacred Moon, but he knew she would get around to it when her thoughts were settled.

When they reached the door to Ben's Emporium Elizabeth said goodnight and went to her quarters. She lighted the lamp and sat in front of it for a while, as a moth or two gathered. She could hardly stir herself when a knock came at the door, and she was tempted to ignore it. But she did not.

"Sheriff Barnes," she said as she saw the big lawman standing there. "Please come in. How is Mr. McRae?"

"Miz Tupelo says he's likely to live, 'less blood poisoning sets in. You can go see him if you want to."

"Is Blue Flower with him?"

Sheriff Barnes was slow to respond. Finally, he muttered a low answer. "Yes, ma'am."

"Then I am not needed."

Sheriff Barnes rose to leave.

"Sheriff, would you take this skirt and blouse to Blue Flower? I'm sure she would welcome a change of clothing."

Sheriff Barnes gathered the clothing in his arms.

"One more thing, Sheriff. I will be leaving for home in the morning. Tell Betsy I will be coming by to get the kitten." Suddenly, a warm smile spread over her face. "The cat will make the place seem so much more like a real home. And when you see Deck, tell him to come along when he's ready. Tell him the bears and spirits are gone."

If you have enjoyed this book and would like to receive details about other Walker and Company Westerns, please write to:

Western Editor
Walker and Company
435 Hudson Street
New York, NY 10014